A *Dire Wolves* MISSION

Savage Security

A Dire Wolves MISSION

ELLIS LEIGH

Kinship Press

Savage Security: A Dire Wolves Mission

First Edition

ISBN

978-1-944336-52-3

Kinship Press

P.O. Box 221

Prospect Heights, IL 60070

Lust is to the other passions what the nervous fluid is to life; it supports them all, lends strength to them all. Ambition, cruelty, avarice, revenge are all founded on lust

— MARQUIS DE SADE

One

Deus moved through the streets, avoiding the pools of light thrown by the streetlamps overhead and sticking to the shadowy stretches. Dressed in dark jeans and a hoodie, he blended into the night well. His choice of wardrobe—the need to disappear into the black—had been an intentional act on his part. His wolf preferred not to stand out, and when the animal instincts he'd been born with bothered to make a judgment against something as trivial as clothing, Deus listened. He'd long since learned never to doubt his inner beast.

The city sat as silent as it ever did, which meant hardly at all, though humans probably couldn't hear the same things he could. Animals scratching their way into garbage bins for their dinners, the scrape of footsteps from people sneaking around in the alleys or hurrying their way past them. The constant droning of television shows, radios singing something soft and sweet, the slow cadence of conversations between friends, and the rough rhythm of fucking—he heard it all coming from the buildings he passed. The city was a veritable symphony of life, bars of birth and death, the bridge of those years in the middle where the majority of living happened. And he…well, he felt more like a spectator than a participant. An audience member watching it all play out.

He preferred it that way, too.

The snick of a lighter caught his attention, and he whipped his head in the direction it originated from. Could be someone enjoying a smoke on their fire escape—could be someone casing an apartment to break in to. Deus was fine with the first, not so much with the second. He didn't fancy himself a vigilante, but he kept his neighborhood relatively safe. Kept an eye on the local riffraff, the con men, and the worse ones. In the six square blocks Deus thought of as his, a woman could walk home without the fear of being raped, though she might get her purse stolen.

Even a thief needed to eat, as he knew well.

By the time he ferreted out the man with the lighter—a neighborhood guy Deus knew by scent and sight outside grabbing a smoke—he was close enough to his favorite Cantonese takeout restaurant to change his path. The neighborhood seemed safe enough, and he could watch the camera feeds he had access to later to make sure. Technically, he'd stolen that access, but he figured it was for a good cause. Like the legend of Robin Hood or some shit—he stole from the rich to give protection to the not-so-rich. He also stole to make a point, stole to pay his rent, and stole to keep his skills at stealing sharp, but those had nothing to do with his neighborhood. Much like a bear, a wolf never shat where it ate.

Bypassing his usual circuit, Deus headed across to the Cantonese joint. It was time to go back to his apartment. He needed a meal in his belly and a few hours of relaxing in front of his screens. Even a quiet city could get on his nerves.

"Ah, Mr. Jones. The usual?"

Deus nodded at the little man behind the counter, taking a spot leaning against the wall. Jones—such an innocuous surname. One he'd picked nearly three centuries before for a birth certificate. All those years later, and he could still use it without fear of being tracked down. There were simply too many Joneses in this country to get very far. First names came and went, but that surname had longevity.

Much like the humans around him, Deus pulled out his phone to pass the time while he waited for his food. A few taps, a quick verification that his VPN was running correctly, and he logged in to his account. Out of habit, he checked his tracking program for his six Dire brothers. Nothing unusual there—everyone seemed to be where they should. Even Luc, their taciturn leader, held steady in some remote Alaskan village Deus had never heard of. Luc had been up there for the past few years, traveling from place to place. Never holding still long enough to make sense. Deus had long since been convinced the man spent his time hunting for something specific, but Luc never confirmed that theory. Hell, Luc never spoke much to begin with.

If anything was wrong, Deus hoped he or his Dire Wolf brothers would know before Luc got himself into the sort of trouble he couldn't get out of. Not that he'd ever been unable to get out of sticky situations. The beast of a man was lucky as hell, but luck only lasted so long. Deus had a feeling Luc's would be running out sooner rather than later.

"Okay, Mr. Jones. That will be thirty-two even." The owner set a bag on the counter and smiled.

Deus handed him a fifty and grabbed his bag. "Keep the change."

Ten minutes and a quick stroll past the park by his house later, he pushed inside his building and headed to the stairs. Humans tended to take the elevators to the upper floors—even in the shorter, squatter pre-prewar buildings that dominated his street—but being trapped inside a moving, mechanical box never had sat quite well with Deus. He preferred to run up the three stories to his top-level apartment. He slipped inside once he reached his door, securing the locks behind him. Wouldn't stop another shifter from getting inside, but the locks would give any human a difficult time. And in the grand scheme of things, humans were far more dangerous than any shifter he knew.

Door secured, he took a deep breath and let the peace wash over him. The calmness. The quiet. *Home,* his human side thought as his wolf echoed him with *den.* Either word fit—they had made it to the place where they were most comfortable. Time to relax.

Shoes off, he padded across the hardwood floors for the living room. The place where he spent most of his time. Deus had fallen in love with his apartment when he'd come to the city for the first time nearly two centuries before. A Jones had lived there ever since, the ownership of the unit passing from one family member to the next. At least, according to the official real estate records.

Big windows overlooking a park, a sweeping view of both open land, trees, and skyscrapers in the distance...and an entire wall of television monitors for him to sit in front of and work. Twelve in total. Perfection for a man in his profession.

Food in hand, he settled into his zero-gravity chair, pulled his worktable across his lap, and looked over each and every screen. Three were broken into different camera feeds from around his neighborhood—some belonging to the city, some to store owners or residents who thought their feed was private, and some from cameras he'd installed as he'd discovered blind spots in his surveillance. Another set played his favorite twenty-four-hour news channel. Nothing interesting there—he'd been through civil wars, world wars, genocides, and population decimation a hundred times over. Fighting was one thing humans tended to excel at, and it was something he'd grown tired of many moons before. Same shit, different day and all that.

A moving dot on another screen caught his attention as he dug into his noodles. Bez—his signature color showed the man in Texas but not at the coordinates for his ranch. His mate, Sariel, wasn't with him, which meant the brother had a job to do. One that would be too dangerous for her. Bez would never let Sariel out of his sight if he could help it. Deus typed a quick note to double-check on that in the morning, as he had nothing on the docket for the shifter. No sense interrupting the man's work, but he'd need to log a report so they all had a record of whatever happened. A history of their pack for when events came back up. Because the thing about history was, it never truly ended or died. It repeated over and over again. You just had to know what to look for.

Deus double-checked the rest of the dots on the screen. All his brothers and their mates were exactly where they should be, save for that one dot indicating Bez off doing whatever he was doing. Deus' pack was safe and secure—nothing out of the ordinary going on. Nothing for him to worry about in terms of protection. Perfect. Time for fun.

The middle screens on his wall displayed three things—a chat forum on the dark web where he found and offered work, the backdoor functionality files of an online first-person-shooter game site he'd built and hosted for a number of years, and the game itself, his player ready to rush into battle in a world he allowed a select few gamers to join him within. Deus settled in, spread his food out on the table before him, and grabbed his keyboard.

"Time to play, fuckers."

As the hours passed, he kept an eye on the dark web chat room. Someone had noticed the completion of a particular job—a transfer of money from very bad, very rich men to not so bad or rich ones. It'd been a long-term heist, taking months to move pennies at a time from hundreds of accounts. The chatters had gotten wind of the fraud and were speculating who could have pulled that off. Deus simply shook his head. He could sniff out undercover federal investigators' usernames faster than most. He wasn't about to brag and draw attention to himself. Besides, even if he did, there was no fucking way they'd find him. He'd buried his info too well, and the dead ends surrounding his screen name were something Deus monitored often.

As the chat moved on—the Robin Hood references growing as people theorized where the money went—Deus kept playing his game. Other players had joined in, but not the one he wanted to see. At least, not until he was on his fourth soda and had already eaten the leftovers from his meal. He'd been in the middle of a particularly tricky part of the game when the name popped up at the right side of the screen. Deus lost his focus, his eyes zeroing in on one word. Birdfoot.

The other players welcomed Birdfoot to the game, joking about why he was late and what he'd been doing. Jacking off seemed to be the consensus, though one gamer threw out that maybe Birdfoot had a date. Typical stuff. But the others didn't know what Deus did.

Birdfoot wasn't a he at all.

Deus couldn't remember the exact moment he'd figured out the player had to be a female. That realization likely came from little things in the style of play, the words she used. The cadence of her sentences. When you were around humans for a thousand years or so, you learned to spot the things people wanted to hide. She wanted to hide her gender and blend in with a room filled with males. Considering how female players were attacked and belittled by their male counterparts, he couldn't blame her, but he had the feeling it was more than simple avoidance of gender stereotypes going on. The question of her reasonings drove him mad, made him focus on her in a way he had never thought about another human before. He didn't know why, but something about her called to him. Made him want to know more. Made him watch for her every night. Made him wonder if she'd ever be up for a little private chat in one of the naughty rooms in the game.

As he contemplated the last time he'd had sex with a woman that didn't involve screens and keyboards—almost twenty years prior at that point—his phone rang with a distinctive tone.

His Alpha.

"What's up, boss?" Deus checked the dots on the map screen, zooming in on where Luc had been hanging out for the past few weeks. Still there. Not moving.

"I need intel on Anuktu, Alaska. It's in the Brooks Range region."

Deus minimized his news screen and pulled up his server. He also opened a browser window and searched that way for the town, just in case the official Dire records didn't show anything. Neither were much help. The place barely existed.

"Population smaller than the staff at Merriweather Fields, no real news stories, pretty well off the grid. What am I looking for here, man?"

Luc growled. "I'm not sure."

That didn't sound like his boss. Deus checked his

screens again almost out of habit, looking for something off. Something to tell him where the problem was. Birdfoot still played, joking with the other guys in the room. She'd also asked where Deus had disappeared to. That was new—her interest in him—but not the sort of distraction he needed right at that second. Later. Definitely later.

"You need backup?" he asked, tearing his eyes away from the woman in question and looking over what little information he could find on Anuktu.

"No. I'm trying to stay as far outside the town as possible to avoid interaction but I need more intel. I'm pulled to the pack out here, and I want to know why."

Luc's intuition was the stuff of legend in his group. The man knew before they did when something was going on in his brothers' lives and whether the something was wrong or right. He'd known about the matings of his five Dire packmates before they'd happened, not that Deus or Luc would ever tell their brothers that. Especially not Deus. Let the men feel only fate could have known about the females in their lives—Luc didn't need the glory of saying he'd seen the women coming. And Deus…well, he knew how much Luc relied on him and only him. There would be no breaking the trust of his Alpha, so the man's secrets were safe in his hands.

If Luc felt a pull to the Alaska pack, there was something wrong with it. A sickness in its midst. The man could sense evil a continent away, and he did everything in his power to eradicate it. Eradicate or inflame, really, depending on his own mood when he arrived. It was the curse of his gift—the dark balancing the light. Too close to evil, and his energy fed it. Too far away, and the sense of it festering ate at him until he exploded. That's where danger lurked…when mistakes could happen. Deus worked his ass off to make sure Luc never made a mistake. Obviously, he needed to work a little harder.

"I'll dig deeper," Deus said, already marking pages and search terms to research.

"Do it fast. Something isn't right up here, and I have no access to anything other than my gut."

In all their years together, he'd never heard Luc so worked up. So…uncertain. "Are you sure you don't need backup? I've got Thaus close enough to you to be there in a few hours, and I can follow him as soon as I can set up a flight."

"No. I've got this one for now. You worry about your world and situation. I'll worry about mine."

Deus' world involved data, coding, and clandestine conversations about wealth and the proper distribution of it. Luc's tended to be more…primitive than that. He preferred tooth and claw to keyboards and data. Something Deus had seen firsthand over the years.

But apparently, not for this job. Or at least, not yet. "Understood. Let me know if you change your mind."

A grunt was the only response he received.

Call ended, Deus dove into research mode. National archives, state history, legends and native histories of the region…anything that might shed light on Luc's premonition needed to be found and examined. A simple story of a ghost in the woods could be the answer they needed, so he delved deep. He'd been a researcher for centuries, long before written records were even kept. He had the skills to search for info and split his attention between that and his game. Not that he was playing anymore, just watching. Keeping an eye on Birdfoot. The girl was kicking ass, and he wished he could be playing alongside her on that run.

He also kept his chat room on the dark web open. People there were still yammering about his heist, some trying to imply they'd perpetrated it. Some claiming it couldn't have happened the way it did. The usual ignorant bravado and sour grapes. None of it important or anything to give much of his attention to.

It was a complimentary post that made him pause, made him stop multitasking and really look at that one screen. What had stood out wasn't the comment itself, though. That honor went to the user's name. Perhaps his senses had been heightened by Luc's call, or the other wolf's intuition had rubbed off on him, but looking at the chat screen, he knew the poster was Birdfoot from his game. She didn't use the same Birdfoot username, but there was something about her phrasing. About the way the words flowed, a pull in his stomach that told him they were one and the same.

A simple two-sentence statement confirmed his suspicion.

"Action is the real measure of intelligence. Whoever thought up this plan had more brainpower than all of you saying it couldn't have been done the way we all know it was."

The same quote—action is the real measure of intelligence—had been typed in a game chat not three months ago. Deus remember being struck by it then, and the feeling hadn't abated. Birdfoot must have read Napoleon Hill. Interesting. A modern woman reading a successful self-help author from the early twentieth century. Not what he'd have expected.

As he dove back into research on the Brooks Range area of Alaska, he couldn't hold back the proud smile on his face. Gamer girl liked his moves. Even his wolf perked up at that thought.

*T**wo***

*G*ood evening, Miss Blake."

Zoe definitely-not-named-Blake stepped out of the car she'd hired to bring her home, steady as ever in the stiletto heels lesser women wobbled in. The ones most women couldn't afford. The doorman held out his hand and helped her to her feet anyway, something she'd always found charming. As if she needed the assistance. As if he were somehow stronger or more physically capable than her. The old man wouldn't last a second against her, but she allowed his kindnesses. It wasn't his fault his human genes and strengths couldn't compare to her wolf shifter ones.

"Good evening, Charles. Busy night?"

"Always, ma'am." He held the door, bowing slightly as he opened the way for her. Such a nice old man. The sort that came from a different time—one she'd lived through. One she remembered a hell of a lot less fondly than the greeting cards and bastardized depictions of history did. Had they met back then, she had no doubt he wouldn't have been nearly as kind, and she wouldn't have controlled her instincts the way she did now. But times changed, and culture moved in new directions, even for wolf shifters like her.

The urge to hunt never did, though.

Easy prey.

Not tonight, beast.

She gave Charles a smile as she passed, keeping the wolf side of herself in check. Not letting the old man see the part of her that would rip out his throat without a second thought if she felt threatened. Nice old men didn't deserve to piss themselves in fear just because her wolf felt feisty.

Zoe strutted through the lobby, her footsteps strong and confident. She'd lived in the revamped former industrial complex—now trendy, high-ceiling loft apartments—for the past three years. She'd gotten to know none of her neighbors but all of the building staff. A lesson learned over many decades honing her craft and refining her style. Neighbors came and went, too busy with their own lives to pay attention to the single woman on the top floor most of the time. But the staff stayed and paid attention. They noticed her odd hours and the animalistic tics that most people disregarded so long as they didn't have to spend a lot of time with her. Humans tended to ignore the threats in their midst instead of dealing with them, a good thing considering how much of a threat she truly was.

But not today. Today, she was just the rich lady in the penthouse suite. Nothing more, nothing less.

She loved the building she lived in—adored the high ceilings, gaudy accents, and reclaimed details from a different time that always brought a smile to her face—but she'd need to move soon. Three years was longer than she usually stayed in one place, and the staff had begun watching her a little too closely. Staying put and falling into a routine meant giving people the chance to catch you doing something inhuman. Zoe had no interest in being caught.

That thought—the idea of being captured and caged—caused something to blow through her mind. Wispy and impossible to grasp. An itch, per se. An instinct so distinctive, even her wolf sat up and took notice. That feeling—that sensation of being uncomfortable in her own skin—usually meant it was time not just to move but to run. Sad, really. She liked Charles and his gentlemanly ways. But she'd learned over the years to trust her instincts, and those instincts were pushing her toward the exit. Soon. Not yet, but soon.

She inserted her key in the elevator and pressed the button for the penthouse. Extravagant, yes. But so damn worth it. Besides, she deserved the finer things in life. She'd certainly suffered through not having them as a child.

Hell, she'd suffered through not having anything, including her freedom.

As soon as the doors opened to her private floor, the stress of the world outside slid away. From the dark wood floors to the soft white walls to the bank of windows wrapping two sides of her living space, the place fit her to a T. Safe and calm and totally hers. Perfection.

She crossed the floor, kicking off her shoes as she went, heading straight for the wall of glass that overlooked the city below. The lights of New York spanned as far as she could see, the borough of Manhattan laid out before her. She loved that filthy fucking town. Loved the greed and the corruption, the simplicity that could be found if you looked hard enough, and the strength of its residents. True, the noise, smells, and sheer volume of humans taking up space every day made her wolf long for open land, but it was easy to disappear in a place like New York. All the hustle, the mayhem. Even a wolf shifter working as a thief could go unnoticed.

Plus, all those distracted humans with shiny things in their pockets, homes, and banks kept her well fed.

Zoe pulled her latest shiny thing from her bag and held

it up, taking her first truly good look at it since she'd stepped off the private jet two hours earlier. Huge, heavy, and worth more than she ever would have guessed, the sapphire and diamond necklace sparkled and reflected the lights of the city across the ceiling. A stunning piece, and one she'd been paid well to acquire. It'd taken her weeks of planning, three full days of prep, and all of twenty-three minutes to steal. Not bad for a mid-six-figure payday.

She stored the necklace in her safe before waking her computer and signing in to her chat account. She needed to send the buyer a message that she'd accomplished her task and set up the exchange so she could get the balance of the fee he owed her. The necklace might have been worth a fortune, but that was only based on what someone would be willing to pay. Zoe didn't openly fence what she stole—it was too easy to get caught. She simply facilitated others acquiring goods. And she was damned good at her job. People got what they wanted through her—all they had to do was hand over some cash.

Message sent, she slipped into her pajamas, grabbed a pint of ice cream from the freezer that had been stuffed full of her favorite flavors, and headed to her living room where three large screens mounted on the wall glowed. Waiting for her.

"Hello, lover," she purred, settling into her chair and grabbing her keyboard. The screens all came to life, different websites popping up on each one. Her workday was over, so tonight she planned on having a little fun. She logged in to her favorite online game, glad to see a few gamers she enjoyed playing with and against already on. This particular game took serious brainpower, and playing with someone who couldn't keep up made her want to rage. No worries about that tonight, though. Even her favorite player, screen name Libidine, showed active and looked to be logging some excellent battles. That guy could really play. If they paired up on a mission or two, her supply and health levels would be maxed in a few hours. Exactly what she needed.

"Time to play, boys." She dove into her game, sticking to her one login for the moment. She had four, even though that was against the terms of service. First, she liked to break rules simply to break them. Second, sometimes she needed to distract some of the younger males in the group. True, the biggest distraction would probably be if she admitted she had a vagina instead of a penis, but she wasn't up for the fallout. She played to relax, not to start World War III with some misogynistic jackass in the Midwest. So she let them swing their dicks around and talk smack in the comments, and she'd join in as another screen name when she needed to distract them, to keep them from playing their best by talking about tits and pussies and the whole *legs for days* and *booty I want to bite* bullshit. Men were easy like that—get their cock involved, and their brains fell out of their shoes.

But her main screen name, the one she'd just logged in to, wasn't there for the bullshit. She was there to win.

Still, she kept another site up on the screen to her right. Kept her dark web message center open as she waited to hear back from the necklace buyer. She'd been expecting a fast response, but that hadn't happened. Something that made her neck itch again. Delays were never a good sign. Maybe he didn't really have the money he'd promised, or perhaps he figured he could knock her off to get her out of the picture and not have to pay at all.

"Or he's sleeping, you big worrywart." Zoe bit her lip and refocused on the game, but her concentration had been shattered. Accepting that fact meant opening another window, this one with her favorite chat room deep within her shady world. Heists from around the world were offered, accepted, completed, dissected, and bragged about on that discussion thread, all hidden away from the rest of the rule-followers and enforcers. It was like a club only a few were allowed entry into, an onion layer only the bravest could peel, and she was one of the few. She'd earned her spot.

Scrolling down the page, she caught one of her favorite ghosts being talked about again. The guy always made the biggest scores in manipulating data and hacking in to systems to slowly, subtly steal from the banks of the super-rich. Money or data—he took it all. While the perpetrator never admitted to the work, never took credit, she knew it had to be the same guy. The style of heist was distinctive, the smoothness of the plan and execution flawless. She'd become a fan of his work, and he'd recently struck again with a month-long data-drive heist that had netted him seven figures. Nice. So she commented on the post discussing the job with a simple message stating how impressed she was. Nothing too telling. And then she went back to her game.

Not five minutes later, a private chat window popped up. Libidine…who'd never spoken directly to her before.

So…you like my heist?

She stared at the screen, trying to put the pieces together. He hadn't pulled off any heists in the game. At least, not that she'd seen. In fact, he'd been a little quiet for the past half hour or so. *What heist?*

The chat rolled on by on the right side, the one not tied to the game. The one about a heist where she'd commented under a different identity.

Her heart began to pound.

No clue what you mean.

She sent the message and sat back, her entire being on alert. Could Libidine and the data heist guy be one and the same?

He confirmed her suspicions by uploading a screenshot of the dark net chat to their game one, highlighting her post.

That's my heist, and that comment is from you.

Fuckity fuck fuck.

Sorry, still no idea.

But she knew exactly what he was talking about, that her days casually playing her favorite game were over, and that it was time to move. She definitely knew all that.

And he knew too much.

So you're the one who snagged the Kuhcaiden Emerald last year.

She froze. That job had been a total secret—a complete lockdown of information coming from both sides. The jewel had been stored in the home of a foreign dignitary in a country the one she claimed citizenship of had been at war with for a few years already. If anyone had found out, she definitely would have been picked up by secret government factions who would make her disappear. No one could possibly know.

But he did.

"Fuck the fates, how'd he put that together?" Zoe stood, pacing, staring at the screens. There was no way she could ignore this. He'd pulled two completely separate aspects of her life together to figure her out, which meant he could know everything about her already. Well, not everything. She doubted there was some sort of data file calling her out as a shapeshifter. That, at least, gave her a modicum of calm. Enough to finally reply.

You keep talking, I keep ignoring.

It was Libidine's turn to go silent. Zoe continued pacing, swinging by the windows to make sure the drapes were closed. She suddenly felt exposed with all those windows she loved so much. Watched. Fucking Libidine, ruining her chill.

The chat room jumped, a new message from him finally appearing.

I don't usually work with anyone, especially not females, but I might for you. I like your style.

With a speed she rarely used on such mundane tasks, she

closed out of all her programs and turned off her computer. He knew…not just her crossover life, but that she was a female. He knew too much. Covers didn't always work. As much as she loved blending into the human world in New York, there were times when her animalness caught someone's attention. Some people were more perceptive than others, or some men decided to stare long and hard at her. She'd grown used to such things, knew how to react and defuse the situation. Knew what to do.

This was different. This was new and, to be honest, both flattering and terrifying at once.

From across the room, her phone pinged. Zoe approached slowly, like a bomb squad moving toward a suspicious package. No way. There was no way it would be him. She refused to believe it…until she saw the screen.

Don't be scared. I won't tell on you so long as you don't tell on me, and if you don't answer me, I'll never bother you again. But if you ever want to pull a job together, the offer stands. Data and physical thievery could be fun. —Libidine

Zoe stared at the message for a solid minute, every scenario she could think of running through her brain. And when she finally landed on the only logical reason behind why Libidine had gone to the trouble to search out her private info, she threw the phone across the room.

"Definitely time to move."

Three

*J*ust like every day that had passed since he'd made what he considered a huge mistake, Deus logged in to the chat room and immediately sought the user info for Birdfoot. Nothing. No updates, no activity. No fucking contact for almost a week, ever since he'd sent that text. She hadn't been in any of the normal hangouts he'd seen her in previously. She hadn't been gaming either. He'd been watching for her to pop up everywhere, but he'd come up empty. He could have cursed himself for being such an idiot—he'd pushed too hard, so she'd gone into hiding.

You'd think after over a thousand years, he'd have figured out how to be less of an idiot around others.

He couldn't even figure out why he'd felt the compulsion to text her as he had. Offering something in person wasn't his style—he liked keeping things online, keeping distance between him and those outside of his pack. He preferred anonymity to social interaction. But something about her had made him want to move their virtual contact into the physical world instead. Which was just plain ridiculous.

"Alaska," he grunted, trying hard to distract himself with other screens so as not to obsess over Birdfoot. "What the fuck is up in Alaska?"

A question he'd been asking himself every day. The town Luc wanted info about was beyond isolated—it sat at the edge of the Brooks Range with no internet presence and no online records database that he could find. The place must have been tech-adverse, which made Deus' job that much harder. He was actually planning to go up there and search out information the old-fashioned way—by talking to people and looking at microfiche files in whatever libraries or historical centers he could find.

The horror.

He was in the middle of contracting a private plane service—one he'd used to fly his brothers around the world at various times in the past—when his phone pinged with a text message alert. He glanced down, cursing the distraction, expecting a message from one of his Dire brothers, but the number came up unknown. The message could have only come from one person, though.

Are you going to hold up your end of the bargain about not bothering me again? Because I really don't want to have to move just yet.

No sign-off, no name. None needed.

No moving necessary unless you want to move to Alaska temporarily for me. I need to do a hands-on job there and would rather skip it. Want to pretend to be me? Are you good with disguises?

He hit send and sat back, waiting. Tapping his foot and rolling his fingers over the trackpad of his laptop for no reason. What was this? Everything about this situation felt new, seemed different. Which, being over a thousand years old, were feelings pretty damn rare to come by anymore. And all the energy building up inside of him, the urge to hunt her down, seek her out, find her. What *was* that? He couldn't decide if he was anxious or afraid, couldn't figure out why he would be either of those things, but he definitely felt some nervous energy coursing through him. An energy that caused him to jump when her reply came.

I'm excellent with disguises but not really a roughing-it sort of girl.

And I'm not really a hands-on sort of guy.

He didn't catch the double entendre in his reply until she responded.

Sounds lonely.

He stared, transfixed. Frozen. Was she…flirting? He grinned at the thought.

I find my ways.

I've heard that about you. Seems you like to play online with people.

Fuck. How could she have heard *that* about him? It wasn't like he got his sexting on often—maybe once a month, if he was being honest. And never under his main username. She'd done her own digging, apparently. Enough so to have found out information on him. That shouldn't have turned him on as much as it did.

Might as well admit to it. Sometimes. Though not nearly often enough to keep me satisfied.

Poor baby. Maybe you need a different partner.

He wished. *Maybe I do. Looking to apply for the gig?*

Depends. What sort of benefits would that entail?

Me. Using every dirty word I know to get you off.

Hmmm…not very enticing.

My vocabulary is huge.

I need more than a big vocabulary.

Meet me in person. Other parts of me are huge as well.

He nearly dropped the phone at that one. Not the hint at his size—the rest of it. He hadn't thought about the words, hadn't really considered them. He'd simply typed what he'd felt and…invited her out. To meet him. Sort of like a human date. Fuck. He didn't date. Never had. Wolf shifters were tied to their chosen mates by some random lottery of fate, so dating really wasn't part of their culture. Sure, shifters would screw around until that perfect someone found them, but not anything like what the humans called dating. No dinners or movies or strained evenings out trying to determine if the lies you told fit with the lies the other person did. Shifters fucked when they needed to scratch an itch—no formal date required. He had to assume she was human, which meant she'd expect him to do human things. Like take her to dinner. And not bite her when he came inside of her tight, hot pussy.

At that thought, and all the ones that involved parts of him inside parts of her, he had to adjust his cock through his jeans. The damn thing was so fucking erect, it had leaked precome all over his belly. From texting. Words on a screen from someone he'd never met. Not the first time that had happened, but definitely the fastest…and least direct.

Hard and wanting and ready to take the girl on as many dinners as he had to, he waited for her response to his offer. And then he waited some more.

The alert that finally sounded from his phone was the ringing of an incoming call, and it wasn't from her.

He swiped to answer, hoping like hell he wouldn't growl into the phone. "What's up, kid?"

Bez grunted a greeting. Or the Bez equivalent of one. "I know Luc's been looking for info on that fucking town in Alaska. How's it coming, old man?"

The only thing that should have been coming was him,

but he tried to tell his cock to stand down. By rubbing his palm over it a time or two. Or six.

"They live almost completely off the grid," Deus said, willing Birdfoot to text again. To respond. To give him some sort of answer so he could think about anything else other than her. "If Luc refuses to go digging in town himself, someone's going to have to go up there."

Deus still hoped it wouldn't be him, especially not if he might have a date to deal with.

Bez squashed that hope quick. "You're the only someone available. How soon can you have boots on the ground?"

Figures. Deus growled, glancing at the screen of his phone to make sure he hadn't missed a message from Birdfoot. Nothing. No response. No date. And now a trip to motherfucking-nowhere Alaska. Perfect.

"I'll book a flight right away. Maybe tonight or tomorrow morning." His voice sounded petulant even to his own ears, something else that irritated the shit out of him.

Clueless as always—or simply ignoring Deus' irritation—Bez said, "Sounds good. Get it done, Deus."

As if he wouldn't. Deus ended the call and pulled up the private plane website again. Changing the details of the flight to make it easiest on him, he booked himself on a trip to Alaska to search out information for Luc. Exactly where he didn't want to be. He also sent one more text to Birdfoot. Because he had no ability to resist her, apparently.

Not in person, then?

She didn't answer right away. In fact, her answer didn't come in for close to three hours. Three very long, very frustrating hours. He'd tried to pass the time with his games, but to no avail. He'd finally given up and headed for the shower, jacking off four times before he finally felt enough relief to get back to work on research.

One ping indicating a text message out of the blue, and he was rock hard again.

Short and direct, Birdfoot's message read *You're quite pushy.*

He couldn't hold back his grin. *And you're quite negligent in replying.*

Maybe because I had things to do.

I was doing *things* while texting you. And afterward. Lots of things afterward.

What sorts of things?

He considered sending her a dirty message but figured the truth would land better. At least, he hoped it would.

Talking to one of my coworkers.

About your Alaska job?

Yeah. Why? You interested in heading up with me? I've got a private plane booked for the trip.

I don't know you.

We can fix that before we get on the plane.

As he'd expected, she gave him another long wait between messages. Every second seemed to span an hour, every minute a full day. And during all of that time, he and his wolf kept their eyes locked on the phone screen. Waiting. Hoping for something. An inch. A maybe. *Something.*

But in the back of his mind, his thoughts turned darker. Warier. He couldn't figure out his reaction to this girl. He didn't date, didn't care to hang around other people, and had no interest in humans. Yet there he was, texting a woman he only knew as Birdfoot to meet up. To fly to Alaska with him. What would he do if she decided to take him up on the offer? He couldn't just come out with "Oh, by the way, I'm an ancient breed of shapeshifter, so don't panic if I turn into a giant wolf with spots on my flank."

He couldn't meet her, couldn't take her with him, and

couldn't continue this flirting thing. He was a fucking Dire Wolf, and she…likely had no clue what that meant.

But when her next text came in, all those instances of he couldn't turned into he would.

When and where?

coffee shop. Such a human place to meet for the first
time, but what could Zoe have said when Libidine
recommended such a public location? "Oh hey, I'll meet you
wherever even if it's private because, as a wolf shifter, I can
kill you in the blink of an eye if you take a single step out
of line."

Yeah, probably not a good idea to lead with that when
meeting a human male for the first time.

Which was how she found herself walking past then
circling around the block and coming back to the designated
coffee shop Libidine had asked to meet her at. She even went
inside and ordered a cup of tea—not because she was thirsty,
but because she wanted to know all the exit points and
corners. She was a big fan of doing recon before a job, and
though she'd never felt the need to do the same in the world
of dating, she figured it couldn't hurt to know the lay of
the land. She didn't spend a lot of time in coffeehouses. She
also didn't meet random strangers from the internet without

having some sort of financial compensation planned for a job. This was all totally new to her.

As soon as she picked the best table for viewing the shop while keeping her back against something solid, her phone pinged. She knew it had to be Libidine before she even swiped to view the message.

You know you can scope out a place without walking into it, right?

Her lips quirked into a smile without her meaning them to, and she shook her head. Jackass.

I prefer to use all my senses, not just what a camera can show me. I'm assuming you're not here yet, unless you have a shock of pink hair like the man in the far corner. Planning on being late?

His response came almost immediately. *No pink hair and no plans to be late. I've got five minutes until our meeting time. Since you're so anxious to meet me, I'll be there in three.*

Zoe took a deep breath, set her phone down in the perfect spot so she could see the screen but he wouldn't be able to when he sat across from her, and sipped her tea. Her leg shook under the table. She was anxious, though not for the reasons she would have expected. She'd enjoyed hookups before—met men for random sex before moving on with the rest of her day. Her meeting with Libidine wasn't like that. There was something about him, even just in his typed messages and his onscreen persona. She felt a pull to him, a need to find out more instead of running away. She had to follow this crazy meeting through to figure out why, and then she could cut him loose and decide what to do next. Move, or kill him? Change all her internet identifications, or tie him up in her apartment for hours of fun?

Such tough decisions.

She straightened her skirt and crossed her legs to keep

from shaking them. Her heels would likely catch some attention, as they were meant to do. There was no mistaking those bright red soles as anything other than designer. She'd picked her entire outfit with care that morning, had spent hours in front of the mirrors trying to look her best without looking like someone trying too hard. She'd chosen the most elegant clothes, the most expensive accessories, and basically draped herself in obvious signs of wealth. Such things scared of plenty of men, the ones who couldn't live up to her expectations. Libidine didn't seem like that type of man, but she couldn't be sure. Many a human male liked to play the part of a person who could afford the finer things in life. She actually could, and no man would get in her way of acquiring the things that filled her with happiness. With comfort. With security.

Zoe knew who Libidine was before he even walked through the door of the shop. Hell, she knew him the second he came into view. Knew his height and the ridges of muscle making up his bulk. Recognized him for what he was. Recognized the lupine grace of his stride. As she watched him approach, her wolf sat up and took notice of the animallike sharpness in his eyes. Yes, they both recognized him. There'd be no need to explain what she was, to tell him about her wolf. He'd know her by scent.

A wolf shifter could always spot one of their own kind.

His eyes zeroed in on hers before he opened the door, and her body went molten inside. Wolf. Definitely wolf, and a powerful one at that. One her own independent Omega wolf would happily spread her legs for. She'd never met a male wolf who could compare with her Omeganess—the source of her inner power.

A gift to most packs, an Omega female could strengthen bonds of the members with ease. When she'd been a child and her mother had recognized the Omega within her, she'd taught Zoe to break those bonds instead so they could run. No use sticking around in a pack that would only use her for her gifts and give her nothing in return. And by nothing, she meant literally nothing. No safety, no comfort, no food, no peace.

But Libidine wasn't from that pack, and he didn't seem to be some weak-minded wolf who would try to cage her in simply to follow someone else's orders. In fact, he seemed almost matched with her in terms of wolf hierarchy. She could sense his strength, could practically smell the fortitude pouring off him as he walked through the door, his steps long but not quick, his stride smooth. She couldn't look away. She'd never once thought about what would happen if she found her mate, but she knew down to the very core of her being that she was about to find out.

With Libidine.

His eyes—so light green, they appeared almost icy— bored into hers as he took the seat across from her, and his lips turned up in a subtle, cocky smile.

"So." That was all he said. One word, but it was enough to send a shiver up her spine. The gritty tone, the deep, rough sound. How could one word make her so wet?

She crossed her legs, hoping he wouldn't notice. Knowing he would.

"So." Zoe took another sip of her tea, holding his gaze the entire time. Her wolf too strong in her own right to back down. "Libidine and Birdfoot."

He hummed. "Lust and Lilith. Interesting connection."

One most people wouldn't have figured out. Hot *and* smart. That combination was almost too sexy to resist.

But she'd try. "So…Alaska, huh?"

God, his grin could stop traffic. "Alaska. Interested?"

Fuck yeah, she was. In him. Not so much in spending time in the frozen north.

She set down her cup and dabbed at the corner of her mouth with a napkin, nearly grinning as his eyes tracked every movement with interest, thankful she'd spent so much time choosing the perfect shade of red. "Depends. What's in it for me? I'm not going to give you all my talents without getting something in return."

The low growl he released shot straight to her clit. He leaned forward, lowering his voice a little as he asked, "What's your name, Beautiful?"

By the fates, if she heard her name in that voice, she'd explode. "You can just keep calling me Beautiful, and I'll call you Alaska."

He laughed, making her want to reach across the table and touch him. Hell, she wanted to do more than touch. She wanted to strip him naked and explore every inch of that body, wanted to sniff and feel and taste him until her wolf felt satisfied that he was hers and hers alone. But she couldn't. Not yet.

Sex with a fated mate wouldn't be some quick tumble in the sheets—it would be permanent in a way she'd always avoided. They could end up tied to each other forever, a thought which cooled her blood quick.

She refused to be someone's kept woman, and she didn't know enough about him to be willing to submit. At all.

Alaska dropped the grin, looking serious again. A lustful fire burning in those cold eyes that had to match the one she found herself fighting as well. "You realize I could find out everything about you with a few internet searches."

Yeah, she knew it. And was surprised he hadn't already done so. "But you haven't, which means you know I won't like it. Besides, what's the fun in stealing some database to find out about me?" She leaned closer, letting her fingers brush the side of his hand. Locking her muscles down tight so he wouldn't see her shiver. "How about you earn what you want instead? I'll tell you my name eventually, if you play your cards right and promise not to go digging into my past."

He sat back, smiling again. Looking so damn handsome, she nearly drooled. "Game on then, Beautiful."

Game on, indeed. "How do you like the city, Alaska?"

And so the afternoon went—both wolves pretending to be human, making small talk as any dating couple would. Meanwhile, her wolf paced in her mind, wanting to move closer to her mate. Craving a physical connection with him. But they kept to the contact to a minimum and the conversation light. Easy. Not revealing too much.

When her phone pinged with an incoming message from the text app she used for her work, she snatched it off the table.

"Everything all right?" Alaska asked. She must have frowned at the message for him to look so concerned. She couldn't help it—the necklace buyer was suddenly ready to meet. They'd given her no explanation for the delay and no options to change the time or location. She only had a couple of hours to prep and get herself across town, which felt rushed. She hated being rushed. Something about the situation felt wrong.

"Beautiful?" Alaska prodded. Zoe shook her head, refocusing on her date with a bright smile.

"Yes, sorry. Everything is…well, it's a little odd but not bad. I do have to leave, though."

"Already?"

Had she not truly needed to leave, his concern would have been a turn-on. She would have invited him home with her and allowed them to give in to their instincts. Carefully—no biting involved.

Instead, she had to go be a thief. "I have another appointment."

As she stood, he growled. Loudly this time. Zoe reacted without thought, placing her hands on his forearms and leaning over him, her face so close to his, she could feel his breath on her skin.

"Stop that," she whispered, glancing around to make sure no one had paid attention to their odd position, to verify none of the humans had gotten scared of the sound of a predator in their midst. "You can't let the humans hear you."

That was when she noticed their positions—how close she'd gotten to him. How appetizing he smelled. How his eyes had specks of darker green along the edges, like the color was fading as it moved closer to his pupils. Ombré, they called that. How he had ombré eyes.

How he couldn't look away from her.

How she seemed to be falling toward him.

How her plan had just gone to shit.

Five

Deus could have counted on one hand the number of people his wolf obeyed. Hell, he could have counted them with one middle finger raised in the air. Only Luc, his Alpha, could wrangle his inner wolf into any sort of submission. Until her. Birdfoot—also known as Beautiful—wanted him to stop, to not scare the humans or do things that were animalistic and could attract attention, so his wolf cut off their growl. Immediately. No questions, no hesitation. The shock of that rocked him to his very core, but the fact that she stood so close, that her scent had surrounded him and was calling him home to her, settled him in ways he'd never experienced before.

This mate shit was no joke.

"I've stopped." Deus leaned forward to run his nose along her jaw, unable to resist. Damn, she smelled good. "Please stay."

A sound close to a whimper escaped her, making his dick practically jump in his pants, and her eyes fluttered as if wanting to close. As if he affected her just as much as she affected him. As if the same lust infiltrating every cell in his body was warming hers as well.

A ping sounded, shattering the moment and bringing tension back to her muscles. The dark-haired beauty with the fiery hazel eyes sighed before taking a step back and reaching for her phone. "I'm sorry, Alaska, but I really can't."

Deus wanted to follow her, to touch her more, to pin her sexy ass against the table and spread her legs. To expose her pussy and eat her like the feast he craved. Like she deserved to be eaten. But the frown on her heart-shaped face stopped him cold. That expression seemed too close to one of concern for him to ignore.

"Something isn't sitting well with you, Beautiful. What is it?"

She smiled, distracted as she typed on the small screen. "Just issues with a client."

"A client you need to meet up with?"

Smile frozen, she darted a glance at him. Wary and guarded once more. "Yes."

His wolf wanted to growl, to drag her back to his den and protect her. But Deus knew instinctually that any move to restrict her would make her bolt, so he chained up his beast and tried to relax. To force his muscles to unclench. To portray a casual sort of calm and interest instead of what was quickly becoming an obsession in his head. "I could go with you, if you like."

She laughed at that offer. Of course. "Not happening. I don't need a babysitter."

"C'mon, Beautiful," he said as he reached for her hand, nearly howling at the spark of electricity that shot through him when their fingers brushed. That sensation, that moment, changed his plans to charm her. He didn't want her to run, but he also didn't have it in him to be cagey about his intentions. Blunt honesty felt like the right way to go in that moment. "I'll be worried about you all night after seeing the way you frown at the messages you're getting. I just want you safe. *We* want you safe."

Her face softened, her body leaning closer as if unable not to. By the fates, she was stunning. So tall and lithe, so strong and confident. He'd been given a gift with her, a blessing he would never ignore. A mate he would spoil senseless.

If she ever stopped long enough to allow him to do so.

Beautiful ran a finger over his hand, making the hair on his arms stand up in attention right along with his cock, before pulling away again. "We'll be fine, but I appreciate the concern. I really do have to leave now."

Fail. But failing at this particular task was okay. A minor setback that wouldn't stop him from getting what he wanted. His mate's refusal to let him into her job that night should have irritated him, but it didn't. He could handle her refusal because he knew he'd eventually work his way all up in her life. He just needed to find a crack in her armor first. Needed to convince her having him around was a good thing.

He needed to get to work.

"Let me walk you out." Deus stood and wrapped his fingers around her elbow, leading her through the crowded coffee shop toward the exit. Keeping her close to him. Not because he worried about the humans around them. No, he simply wanted her body next to his. Wanted to smell her heady feminine scent, wanted to feel the warmth of her. He held on all the way across the room and to the doors leading to the street. He didn't let go when they got outside either. Something she definitely noticed.

"Are you always this clingy?" she asked, still allowing him to hold on to her. To lead her. To be close to her.

"Only when I find the one woman the fates declared as my perfect match."

"Yes, well, the fates have been known to be wrong."

He couldn't hold back his smile—that sassy tone both challenged and intrigued him. Fuck, he hoped she used it in the bedroom. "Perhaps. But not this time."

"How are you so sure?"

"Even without having met you, I've been slightly obsessed with you for a year. Tell me, Beautiful, have you been watching my exploits? Tracking my online persona?" When she remained silent, he pushed a little more. "Be honest, now. You've felt the same need to keep up on what I'm doing as I have to check in on you. And it's been getting stronger every day."

"Ridiculous." But she didn't sound as if she believed that. In fact, she sounded a little stunned. As if she was finally putting pieces together in her head. Figuring things out.

"It's worse now that we've met," he said, pulling her closer. Needing to feel her body against his. To bring her close enough so he could whisper in her ear. So they could be alone right there on a crowded street in the middle of the day. "You're aroused, Beautiful. I can smell it. You want me to touch you more, to press my lips against yours, to dip my hands under that tight little skirt and spank your naughty pussy. You want my cock."

She huffed and pulled her arm from his hold, her face flushed and her breaths coming fast. "That means nothing."

She doth protest too much. "It means we have a connection."

"Sure...a physical one." She stalked closer, letting her wolf lose a little. Letting him see the power of her beast. "Just because we want to feel your cock inside us doesn't mean we want a single thing more. Our connection is flimsy, our attraction based on lust. I don't have time to help you get your rocks off right now, though."

The growl he released rumbled through his chest and

definitely attracted the attention of passersby, but Deus was too far gone—too fucking angry—to hold it back.

"You think I need your help to get off? You think that's the only thing I'm worried about right now? Wrong, princess. Yes, I want you. Yes, I want to strip you naked. But not just so I can—how'd you say it?—get my rocks off. I want to spoil you. I want to worship your body the way it deserves to be." Deus pulled her closer, letting her feel how she affected him. Letting her get a good look at the desire in his eyes as his wolf peered through them. "Our connection may be based on lust right now, but it's far from flimsy. And when I get you alone finally, when I have you spread out before me and you allow me access to this tight little body, it'll be you getting your rocks off. Multiple times. Fuck, Beautiful—I'm going to make you scream when I get my hands on you. When I finally get to taste what's between those sexy-as-fuck legs of yours." A little closer still, every breath she took pressing her breasts against his chest. "But none of that can happen if you're dead."

She blinked, her body going stiff. He held her stare with his, pinning her with it. Making sure she understood. That she knew he wasn't fucking around.

And she did. He could see it in her eyes, feel it in the energy around her. Not that it mattered. His mate was nothing if not stubborn.

"I need to get to work," Beautiful said, pulling herself away from him. Forcing distance between them. Leaving him standing there on the street alone. She had only taken a few steps before stopping and turning back to face him. "It's a simple handoff—I'm worried about getting paid tonight, not dying."

"Yeah, well…that makes one of us."

Her lips quirked up. "Your concern is touching. Unnecessary, but touching. Good day, Alaska."

"Good day, Beautiful." Deus watched her walk away, his wolf growing more agitated with every step.

Before she disappeared into the crowd, she turned one last time and shot him a glare that would have made a lesser man's knees shake. "And don't even think about tracking me tonight."

He totally thought about tracking her. And as soon as he made it home, he planned it out and enacted it too. Followed her through traffic cameras and various other CCTV feeds he hacked in to along the way to verify where she lived, then set up a ring of cameras to keep an eye out for her exit. The job wasn't perfect—her building wasn't in his neighborhood so he had trouble with blind spots—but it gave him something to do instead of panicking over her being ambushed by some client.

Deus waited for almost an hour for something to come up, the fear that he'd somehow missed her exit twisting his gut. And strengthening his resolve. The next time he saw his mate in person, he was putting a tracker on her damn phone. Fuck it—he needed her to be safe more than he needed her to not want to kill him.

The ringing of his own phone had him diving for it, but he could only sigh when he saw his Alpha's name on the screen. Not who he wanted to deal with at the moment. Which definitely showed as he growled out his greeting. "What?"

"Easy, son." Luc's low rumble made the hair on the back of his neck stand up, his Dire power working its way over the connection. "I can feel your stress from here and I know you're distracted, but I wanted to check on when you're coming to Alaska."

Shit. Deus glanced at the time—he didn't have enough of it to make the flight he'd booked. Didn't really matter—no fucking way could he leave his mate behind without knowing she was safe. He didn't want to leave her behind at all. And Luc, having been through this with five packmates already, would understand that need once he knew the fates had finally gifted Deus with a woman like Beautiful.

Which was not a conversation to have right then. Instead, while typing a quick rescheduling note to his pilot, Deus responded, "First thing tomorrow. I booked a private plane."

For two, but Luc didn't need to know that just yet.

"Good. I'm going to need you to…"

But his Alpha's words faded out as Deus finally saw what he'd been waiting for. He almost didn't recognize his sexy mate as she left her building. She seemed hidden under a long, thick fur coat and a pair of sunglasses so dark and round, they covered half her face. His Beautiful…disguised. And leaving.

Time to focus on tracking her.

As she stepped into a waiting car, Deus did the only thing he could. He told his Alpha, "I'll call you back," and hung up his phone.

The car with his mate in it took off down the street, speeding across town while he watched. The chase definitely on. Deus switched from screen to screen, camera to camera, to keep the vehicle in his sights. Right turn, left…losing it at one point but picking it back up two blocks down. His surveillance felt like a game of *Frogger*, the focus of every ounce of his attention bouncing all over the roads as each camera caught a glimpse of the vehicle she rode in. As he jumped from feed to feed to follow her.

Finally, the car pulled alongside a curb and pulled to a stop in a neighborhood he wasn't really familiar with. She stepped out and looked around, her movements slow and precise. Her eyes still blocked by those damn sunglasses. He had a decent shot of her, but the focus was from the back, so he took to another screen and checked the feed from camera to camera, trying to get a shot of her face. A direct look at her expression instead of some side view. He needed to see her, to get a feeling of if she was confident or nervous.

His phone rang, but he ignored it, focused wholly on seeing what his girl was up to. But when she turned, when he saw her arm raised as if holding something to her face and his phone rang again, he figured it out.

"Beautiful?" he asked as soon as he swiped to answer her call.

"Are you watching me?"

"You told me not to." Not a lie—not an answer to her question either.

"Doesn't mean you listened."

He could hear the smile in her voice, so he simply chuckled.

"You're a naughty boy, aren't you, Alaska?"

Yes. Always. "I *am* a bad listener. You should probably be aware of that fact."

"Good to know, and I'm glad for it right now. I need you to pay attention. Something isn't right with this job."

Every bit of humor disappeared, and when he spoke again, his words came out on a rough growl. "What can I do?"

"You can see me now?"

"Yes, turn a little to the left." Fuck, that pretty face made his gut clench and his cock hard. "Gotcha—camera must be on a light pole because I'm looking down on you."

"I see it. Do you have access to any cameras inside the building across the street by chance? The one under construction."

Deus scanned the immediate area for CCTV feeds and

any sort of electrical patterns that would indicate extended security cams, coming up empty. Mostly. "No, but I've got surveillance pointing toward the building from the north side and have a great view in."

"Anything stand out on floor six?"

He counted up the windows and searched, zooming in as much as possible and cursing the grainy, black-and-white footage. "Nothing that I can see, but you've got company on seven."

"Brilliant."

He didn't see how people possibly lying in wait for her could be anything but a threat. "Don't move, Beautiful. I can be there in five."

"No need." She took off her coat, revealing a slick, skintight leather jumpsuit that had to have come from some of Deus' own fantasies. She'd tied her hair up in a slick ponytail and wore much more sensible shoes than she had that morning. Fuck, she looked good. If she made it out unscathed, he was going to spank that tight little ass for days. A thought that had him groaning and sinking deeper into his chair. He couldn't help himself. He slid a hand down to his rock-hard cock and pressed, looking to relieve the ache she ignited in him.

"What are you doing, naughty boy?" she asked, her head cocked to the side and her brow drawn down in question. He must have groaned out loud. No sense lying about it.

"Your ass looks amazing in those pants. I was just thinking about spanking it, but I think I'd rather give it a bite or two."

"You really *are* naughty, aren't you Alaska?" She blew a kiss to the camera. "We'll talk about spanking and biting another time. I'm off to deal with the boring part of my job, though this one seems a little more interesting than most. Thanks for the heads-up."

Before he could say another word, she ended the call, tucked her phone into her bra, and headed into the building. Out of his sight. Frantic, cock forgotten, he opened every feed in the area, taking up each screen on his wall. Searching for anything—a glimpse, a shadow, a view through a window. Anything at all. But the cameras gave him nothing.

"C'mon, Beautiful. Show me your face." He enlarged the video feed from the north side of the building, checking every window. Scanning and rescanning. Five minutes. It would take him five whole minutes to make it to that part of town in his human form, and he'd have to go human. It was too early in the evening to get away with running through the city in his wolf form. That frustrated him to no end. He should have left when he offered, should have ignored her refusal. Sure. She was a wolf shifter like him and could likely take care of herself in a fight, but a bullet to the head would kill a shifter just as quickly as a human. She was his mate, *his*. The need to protect her overrode everything else.

Suddenly, Deus spotted movement, his eyes seeking her out and finally finding her. She'd somehow made it up to the eighth floor and was creeping across to what looked like a stairwell still under construction. Seven men stood in the room below her, though none close to the stairwell. There could have been more men on the floor—he didn't have a clear view. He cursed himself for not giving her a head count. He had no way to let her know what she was walking into, how many adversaries she'd have to deal with. He could only hope she'd be prepared for such a large group.

Okay, not only hope for *that*. Because two of the men were definitely armed. His second hope would be that they didn't have great aim. Five. Fucking. Minutes. Away.

His girl snuck down the stairs and around a corner, coming up behind the group of men. Deus leaned forward, literally on the edge of his seat. Watching. Waiting. Every inch of him ready to dive through the screens and come to her rescue.

With speed the likes of which he'd rarely seen, she took down all seven. No real struggle, no stress. Easy. Fast. Seven dead humans without breaking a sweat or letting one of them get a shot off. There was no way she wasn't an Omega wolf—a powerful female of his breed. His mated packmates had all ended up with Omegas, so the fact that Beautiful carried that same innate power didn't surprise him. The fact that the fates had gifted him someone like her totally did. Good goddamn, she impressed him. Even more so when she stepped right in front of a window on the north side of the building and waved. To him.

"Sassy," Deus grumbled, snagging a screenshot of that little wave before finally relaxing into his seat. He watched as she headed for the stairwell again, her head high and her ass swaying. Completely confident. Completely prepared for whatever would come her way. Amazing.

Ten minutes later, Beautiful walked out the front door of the building, those huge sunglasses back in place, a small bag thrown casually over her shoulder, and not a scratch on her delectable body. The driver met her at the car, helped her into her fur coat, then held the door for her. Simple and quick, efficient. And something no human would pay attention to in a city like New York. Brilliant. He waited until the driver had her secured in the car to call her, smiling when she picked up.

"Yes, dear Alaska?"

"Job accomplished?"

"Of course. Everyone has to pay the piper, and today, that means me. But you didn't call to see if my client came through with his payment.

No, he didn't. Balls to the wall time. "Come do this job in Alaska with me. I've booked a jet. We can have some fun in the snow."

"I hate the cold."

"You have a fur coat. Two, at least, from what I've seen."

Her sigh sounded both irritated and completely phony. Damn, she was fun.

"What do I get out of this?" she asked, and Deus knew he had her. She'd be on the plane with him in the morning.

"Me."

"Not enough."

He'd make sure it would be, but he could play her game. "What do you want?"

She hummed, taking forever to answer him with a casual, "A favor to be named later."

A dangerous proposition, going in without knowing the exact terms. Not that he had to think twice about it. "Deal. I'll text you the details. And, Beautiful?"

"Yes, Alaska?"

"Don't be late."

"You wouldn't leave without me."

No, he wouldn't. But he'd never tell her that.

Hell, he didn't need to. She knew.

Six

The car Zoe had hired to take her to the airport rolled onto the tarmac and headed for the plane parked in front of a large, silver hangar. The small airport in New Jersey Alaska had directed her to was one she'd never visited before, though she didn't exactly fly often. Her wolf tended to get uncomfortable in small spaces filled with humans. But this? This would be different. This flight would be only her and Alaska, with a small crew as far as she understood.

It would also be very expensive, which wasn't something to ignore. If Alaska had been trying to impress her with his casual *I've booked a jet* comment, he'd succeeded. Not that Zoe would let him know that so easily. As much as she liked to spend money, she'd never flown on a private plane. Today would be a first for her, and she was definitely looking forward to it. She'd hardly slept the night before, too anxious and excited to turn off her mind. She was flying to Alaska…with Alaska. Her fated mate and a man she barely knew anything about. Traveling with him for an indeterminate length of time and to a location he hadn't even told her about yet.

Zoe still couldn't believe she'd agreed to any of this.

The sky burned peachy gold, sunrise only half an hour past as she stepped out of the car. Alaska stood leaning against a black SUV, sunglasses on and legs crossed at the ankles as he checked his phone. He looked good enough to eat in his dark jeans and sweater, with his floppy dark hair being ruffled by the breeze. He also looked like a model for one of those higher-than-middling chain clothing stores all the "good" malls across America housed—casual, collected, and completely absorbed by whatever played out on the screen in his hand.

Time to distract him.

"Is there a problem?" Zoe asked, adding a little extra swing to her hips when he looked up. Alaska smiled, pulling off his sunglasses, looking from her stiletto heels to her leather miniskirt to the low-cut cashmere sweater she wore. She'd wanted to appear sexy but touchable, and if the gleam in Alaska's eyes when he tucked his phone into his pocket was any indication, she'd succeeded.

"No problem now that you're here." Alaska pushed off the car and stepped closer, his loose-hipped gait exaggerated by his long, thick legs. Zoe locked her knees and pressed her thighs together, not wanting to give away how much she wanted him already. Seconds…that was all it took for him to ramp up her arousal and make her wet. Soaked even. Her inner wolf was a total slut for him in the best possible way. But Zoe couldn't let her beast loose, couldn't give in to the need burning bright inside of her. She needed to keep a little distance between them, no matter how much her wolf fought that plan.

It was going to be a long flight.

Alaska stopped right in front of her and ran a finger over her cheek, still smiling. Still looking so damn handsome, it hurt. "You're extra beautiful this morning, Beautiful."

She rolled her eyes at his horrible play on words yet

couldn't be anything but honest. "I was just thinking the same thing about you, actually."

His grin flashed bright and wide. "Yeah?"

"Yeah." She nodded at her driver as he placed her bags at her feet. "Now, is all that muscle just for show, or are you going to be able to carry my bags for me?"

He growled low, inching closer before shooting her a wink. "Carl?"

Zoe frowned until a man in a black suit and mirrored shades stepped beside Alaska. A human man.

"Sir?"

"Load the lady's bags, please." Alaska cocked his head, still watching Zoe as Carl grabbed the bags and carried them up the stairs and into the plane.

"You have a human to do your heavy lifting?" Zoe asked, keeping her voice pitched low. Unable to put even an extra inch between them.

As if feeling the same way, Alaska wrapped an arm around her waist and pulled her toward the stairs leading up to the cabin. Staying right beside her. Touching all the way. "Technically, I have a pilot who's happy to take my money and load your bags. But whatever you want to imagine him as, I'll go along with it."

"So you're not the one flying today? Pity. I had all these fantasies about me and you and your cock...pit."

Alaska growled, his hand sliding down to her hip. His body crowding hers. "Beautiful, you can definitely hang out on my cockpit all you want, but I'd prefer to be alone with you when that happens."

"Opportunity trumps preferences every time."

"Well, I plan to give you plenty of opportunity to take advantage of me. We've got a long flight ahead of us. Plenty of time for whatever it is that devious mind has planned."

His hand slipped into hers, their fingers weaving

together as they climbed the stairs to the plane. It was such a sweet gesture, such a simple one. Something she'd never experienced. Something that softened her heart and made her want to purr her happiness. Made her want to hold on to him forever.

But as she stepped inside the plane, he let go. She had about half a second to miss the warmth of his hand in hers before a sharp crack sounded. Zoe jumped as Alaska's hand landed squarely on her ass, her body both wanting to run away from it and beg for more at the same time. His devilish grin when she spun to face him—eyes likely wide and mouth probably hanging open—didn't help her situation.

"Did you just spank me?"

"I told you what I wanted to do to that ass. First one accomplished—we'll talk about the biting once we're in the air." He herded Zoe toward the leather seats, grinning down at her. So big and powerful and male. So hers. "Take a seat, Beautiful. The temptation of giving that phenomenal ass another smack is almost too much for me to resist."

"I knew you were a naughty one."

He chuckled. "You have no idea."

Maybe not, but she wanted to. Badly. Had she thought the flight would be long? Between the lust in his eyes and the way her body was responding to him, she had a feeling it wouldn't be long enough.

— —

Two hours. Zoe made it two hours into the flight before cracking. Alaska had made sure she was comfortable before takeoff, had even teased her a little with a soft kiss to her cheek and a hand on her thigh, but then he'd broken out his laptop and started typing away. She'd watched him for a bit, wondering if he was in the middle of planning one of his internet heists. Wondering how those thick fingers would feel working her body the way they worked the keyboard. Wondering what the hell she was doing flying to Alaska with a stranger.

A stranger the fates thought was a perfect match for her.

Could they be right? She had to admit, she was attracted to him. Hell, what women wouldn't be? Tall and thick and so fucking handsome it seemed impossible that he didn't have women throwing themselves at him on the daily, the man exuded the sort of confidence that pulled people in. And those eyes. Every time they flicked her way, that they caught her staring, the heat built within her. So light, so unusual. And the way they showed his hunger whenever they met hers—so fucking amazing. The man didn't need to say a single word when he looked at her that way.

Which was why she felt so proud to have made it two full hours without demanding his attention. But even she had a limit…and she'd hit it.

"Alaska's a big state, you know," Zoe said, pretending to be focused on a game on her phone.

He jerked, his head popping up and his brow tightening. "What?"

"Alaska," she said, drawing the word out. "It's big. And you never told me exactly where we're going."

He cocked his head, looking at her with much more interest. Making her want to squirm in her seat or crawl into his with him. Her self-control had no chance against that man.

"You must trust me an awful lot to get on a plane and fly off with me when you have no knowledge of our exact destination."

She could play the sarcasm card just as well as he could. "Don't count on it, Alaska."

He grinned, and that look—that moment of happiness

on his face—stunned her. Made her lose her ability to speak. And think. And…do stuff. The bastard.

Alaska typed for a moment, then turned his laptop around so she could see the map on the screen. The map of Alaska, of course.

"We're headed to the Brooks Range—just north and east of the Anaktuvuk Pass. There's a pack of wolf shifters there that we need information on."

Pack. An icy splinter shot straight up her spine at the thought of what sort of pack they might be heading toward. "And you can't get that information from them from New York?"

He frowned, turning his computer around again and closing the lid. "They're…slightly off the grid."

That pause. It meant something more than he might have intended it to. The delay felt important. "How slightly?"

"The kind of slightly that requires an in-person trip."

"So…the slightly that really means completely."

"Pretty much."

Huh. That sounded the opposite of the sort of place he'd ever want to be. Her as well. "So there's no data to delve into, no internet footprint, and no way to know what's going on without infiltrating this pack. That must drive you crazy."

His eyes burned as they caught hers. "You have no idea."

Zoe sat back, crossing her legs as her mind swirled. What on earth could they possibly want with a pack out in the middle of nowhere? There couldn't be much to gain from them. Maybe some gold or oil rights, though that really wasn't the sort of thing Alaska had gone after since she'd been aware of him. They weren't his preferred targets. He dealt in internet theft—taking from those with more than they needed. If the pack had no internet life, assumedly no money, and no status, then…

"What's the prize?"

Alaska gave her another confused look. "Prize?"

"The end goal of the game. What are we investigating some nothing pack for? I can't see the prize."

"No prize. My boss wants info and can't find it himself, so I'm going to get it for him."

Boss. Something about that word made the hair on the back of her neck stand up. Zoe prided herself on being able to read people, and right then, she read Alaska as someone avoiding a topic. If she let her imagination take over, she'd say he was dodging something about their situation. He'd chosen *boss* specifically—an innocuous, bland sort of word. Alaska wasn't bland.

He also wasn't telling her the whole truth.

She picked up her phone again and concentrated on the screen as she let her mind wander. As she contemplated whether she should have trusted him or not. The fates had thrown the two of them together, and while she had to admit her physical attraction to him consumed most of her thoughts, she didn't have to let anything happen. She could leave the bond incomplete, refuse the mating. She could walk away at any point...unmated, unclaimed.

Independent.

Alone.

A thought that had never bothered her before she met him.

*S*even

*I*s there anything else, sir?"

Deus nodded to Carl, who stood just inside the cockpit. "Not today. Stay local, though. I'll call if we need you before our scheduled departure."

"Whatever you need, sir. Enjoy Alaska, ma'am." Carl nodded to Beautiful, who seemed focused on what was outside of the plane instead of inside it. Deus couldn't blame her. There was something about the air in Alaska that reminded him of home. Not New York home or even United States home—ancient home. The place where he'd been born. Where he'd been part of his first pack, where he'd first met Luc and Bez. Hell, that place didn't even exist anymore, centuries of war and disputes over borders destroying the land he'd first explored as a young wolf causing boundaries and names to shift. He could barely remember the place any longer, hardly pick it out on a current map, but he'd never forget the scent of the forest the first time he ran as a wolf with his pack. The cold, crisp, clean air within the Arctic Circle definitely tugged at those memories.

Deus helped Beautiful down the stairs from the plane, watching her face as she took in the sights. Mountains, trees, and snow as far as the eye could see in front of them, two metal buildings with rounded roofs behind them, and a single unpaved road leading out of the field the region thought of as an airport. Not exactly a bustling metropolis, and nowhere near good enough for a woman like her. She looked like a million bucks, far more than the entire damn town was likely valued at.

"Are you warm enough?" he asked once their shoes hit the runway. Though that term could only be applied loosely—there was no paved landing area, just hard-packed dirt and snow. Completely basic but functional. And nowhere near what she was probably used to.

"I'm just fine, thank you." She smiled, those bright red lips lifting just enough to tempt him, and his world tilted on its axis. He hated feeling so off-kilter, but his wolf loved this. Loved having her close, seeing her facial expressions change as he took in her scent. Loved that out-of-control falling feeling of being anywhere near his fated mate. Deus...well, it might take him a little longer. He didn't quite trust her yet, a fact made evident when she'd asked why they were coming to Alaska. He'd gone with *boss* instead of Alpha for the person who needed help. Something that ate at him a little—the entire statement had not really been a lie, but not the whole truth either.

The wording had come naturally, like an instinct to protect his own, and he couldn't say he regretted the choice. He'd make the same decision again if he needed to, but that didn't mean he liked it. She was his mate—his forever—and he wanted to tell her all about his pack and his life and his Alpha. Just...not yet. His pack's safety came first still. His Alpha's safety definitely had to come first on this trip. But even that wasn't the true meaning behind his subterfuge.

She had no pack, that much was obvious. Whether that was intentional—some wolves chose a nomadic lifestyle—or not was left to be determined, but it didn't matter. If she had no pack, she likely didn't want one. Which meant she wouldn't want *his* pack involved in her life. No matter how non-pack his group was.

Mentioning *Alpha* or *pack* seemed wrong in regards to his brothers. Luc wasn't your typical Alpha, and their pack was more than a little unusual. Most shifters didn't even know the legends of the Dire Wolves anymore—his breed had been *extinct* for centuries. Yet he and his six brothers had survived, forming their own unconventional pack and spreading across the country known as the United States. They'd believed they were the last Dires left, though they'd recently discovered that likely wasn't true. Something they needed to investigate as soon as Luc was finished in Alaska. Still, they worked at supporting the North American Lycan Brotherhood leader when he needed more force or intel than a regular shifter could get him, but mostly they kept to themselves. And they kept the mystery of their lineage a tightly held secret.

Deus wasn't ready to tell Beautiful all that yet or risk losing her over something so loosely defined. But trust her or not, he was more than ready to get his hands on the curves that had been torturing him the entire flight.

"So," she started, still looking out over the mountains before them. "What now?"

I pull you underneath me and fuck you until you break.

"Luc said he'd be sending a local wolf to pick us up and bring us to town once we landed. I expect the guy will be here any minute."

"Do you need to call him or something?"

He spread his arms wide. "There's nothing here, Beautiful. I'm pretty sure anyone in a five-mile radius knows a plane just landed."

She scowled, her lips turning down in what he

could never tell her was an adorable sort of expression. "Smartass."

But as he'd expected, a truck soon came rolling over the snow toward them. Deus stood next to Beautiful, watching the approach. Suddenly uncomfortable at the thought of sharing space with another male...and his mate. Another instinct he wasn't prepared for—the one that spoke of ownership. The one to claim, to squirrel her away and keep her safe. The one that demanded he rub himself all over her body so she smelled like him everywhere.

Soon, wolf. Soon.

The truck came to a stop in front of the plane. Deus watched carefully, moving his body to stand between his mate and the vehicle. Ready to defend her if necessary. He'd seen her fight off humans—he doubted his overprotectiveness was necessary. But there was no convincing his wolf of that.

"Luc sent me. You Caleb?" the unknown shifter said as he stepped out of the truck. Deus nodded, responding to the name he'd chosen to go with on this mission, not missing the way the other male's eyes darted to something behind him—to Beautiful. "Who's the female?"

Beautiful stiffened for a moment then moved closer to the man, smiling and jumping in before Deus could respond. "The name's Beautiful, and I'm here with this big lug."

The male eyed Deus, practically challenging him. "Fitting name."

Deus couldn't hold back the possessive growl or how his hand moved to Beautiful's elbow to pull her closer. To protect her. To make sure this guy knew she belonged to him. "We're here to work, not flirt."

Hands up, the wolf gave Deus a sarcastic sort of smile. "No harm, friend. She didn't smell claimed."

She wasn't, so Deus kept his mouth shut. Beautiful pulled her arm out of his hold and directed a raised eyebrow at him, as if waiting for him to say something. Apologize, perhaps. Wouldn't fucking happen, but she didn't know that. Or maybe she did, because that look grew darker, harder. More dominant. He nearly whimpered under her gaze, his wolf wanting to give her anything she needed. The man in him knowing he'd only stick his foot in his mouth if he tried. For that particular battle, the man won out. At least, until Beautiful turned away from him with a huff, obviously pissed.

He definitely whimpered at that.

As the stranger grabbed their bags and loaded them into the back of the truck, Beautiful sent another paint-stripping glare at him and whispered, "Your name is Caleb?"

Okay—so she wasn't mad enough to miss that particular detail. Deus took her attentiveness and willingness to ask him a question at all as a good sign.

He shot her a wink and a smile. "For this trip, it is."

"Damn," she said, keeping her voice soft. Still close enough for Deus to get slightly lost in the scent of her. "I thought I had you."

Unable to resist, Deus leaned closer, brushing his lips against her ear as he breathed, "Beautiful, you can have any part of me you like. For as long as you like. As many times as you like."

She backed away and gave him a sultry smile, her eyes flicking down to the erection pressing against his zipper. "I'll take that under consideration. But payback is a bitch, you know."

He did, though he had no clue what she meant.

At least, not until she hopped into the truck—sitting squarely in the middle of the bench seat between him and the male wolf who'd come to pick them up. Once the three of them were trapped inside the tight quarters, she pulled out her inner flirt and released it. At the other male.

"What's your name, handsome?"

The guy shot Deus a cocky look before turning his hungry gaze on Beautiful. And because she'd placed herself between them, because she was the one turning her body toward the other male and paying him the attention Deus craved, he had to let her. She'd never forgive him if he pulled her away or tried to overtake the conversation. She was already pissed at him—he didn't need to make that worse.

There was nothing he could do but sit, listen, and try his hardest not to growl out his jealousy.

This trip was going to be the death of him.

Eight

$\mathcal{C}$harlie—the male wolf who'd picked them up from the airport and had a serious propensity for staring at Zoe's breasts while he should have been driving—dropped them off at a cabin deep in a spruce forest along what no one in their right mind would have called a road. The little wooden building sat alone among the trees, well past rustic and heading straight for uninhabitable. But Charlie promised that it was fully outfitted for two wolves to be comfortable for up to a month.

Zoe had a feeling his idea of comfort and hers were from two totally different worlds.

"Watch out for the local pack. They're not as friendly as I am," Charlie said with a leer just before he headed back to his truck. "There's an old Jeep in the outbuilding you can use and plenty of wildlife around. If you need anything at all, Beautiful, you come see me. I can take care of you."

Zoe stood and waited, watching as he drove off toward the highway. Keeping a smile pasted on her face and her back to Alaska. Making a point.

As soon as his truck disappeared from view, though, her smile fell and she shook my head.

"Right," she said, drawing out the word. "As if there's any chance of that happening."

"I wonder what he meant about the local pack."

She shrugged, too absorbed in the feeling of needing a shower after the way Charlie had assaulted her with his eyes to filter her words. "Never trust a pack wolf."

Alaska went silent and stiff, staring at her with a blank expression on his face. "You're anti-pack."

She stared back down the road, watching Charlie's taillights grow smaller. "Whether I am or not isn't important. Charlie definitely was."

"He was also interested in you."

"He doesn't know me—he just liked what he saw."

"It must be hard to be such a people person."

Zoe spun, unable not to stare. Not to notice the confidence that rolled off him, the fire burning in his eyes. The way her wolf responded to his closeness.

"Pardon?"

He shrugged, casually sexy with every move he made. "You're stunning, Beautiful. Any man can see that—but it's not the only thing we're attracted to. You're engaging, and when you give people your attention, it's like the sun shining down and warming them. It's hard to walk away from that." He grabbed her bags and leaned in close, his breath brushing her cheek as he murmured, "If it were me in Charlie's spot, I'd have offered too. Hell, I *have* offered."

He had. A few times. And she knew it wouldn't be much longer before she gave in and accepted. Before she gave her body to him in pleasure. It wouldn't be long at all. Especially if he kept speaking so sweetly about her.

With another one of those winks that made her thighs clench and her panties wet, Alaska headed inside, carrying all their luggage. "Are you coming with me or not?"

Coming before you, with you, after you…however I

can come. She kept her dirty thoughts to herself, though. "Totally."

Inside, the cabin was about as small as Zoe had expected. There were no rooms, just one big open space with what looked like a bathroom in the back corner as the only separated section. A couch, a rocking chair, a two-person dinette, a single dresser, and a bed barely big enough for the two of them without sharing some serious physical contact made up the furniture. The more she took in, the longer she stared at the construction and details, the more her skin itched. Everything about the place reminded her of the cabin she'd grown up in. Every single detail. That couldn't be a coincidence, and this wasn't just some random cabin in the woods.

This was the house of a pack wolf—one given to newly mated couples.

She suddenly felt sick to her stomach.

"Coffee?"

She jumped, swallowing hard when she met Alaska's concerned gaze. Fighting to hold back the sick rising in her throat. "What?"

He raised an eyebrow and held up a mug. "I was going to make some coffee. Would you like a cup?"

Coffee. Right. Normal. Totally normal. Damn it, she needed to pull herself together. "Yeah. Sure. That'd be great."

Her mate continued to watch her, his gaze practically assaulting her already anxious mind. She stood firm, though. Strong. Refusing to break in front of him. Refusing to give in to the anxiety growing inside of her at being *back*. Not the same place, not even the same state, but the same type of life. Of expectations and gnawing emptiness when they weren't met. The same hell she'd escaped.

Finally, Alaska released her gaze to turn and move through the kitchen. Making coffee on the stove. Something she'd seen her mother do a thousand times for Zoe's father. Something that only made her pulse pound harder.

"What's got you on edge, Beautiful?" Alaska asked, not even looking at her. A move that definitely seemed intentional. He was trying not to crowd her. To give her enough space so she could calm herself. She appreciated that fact, even if her assumption might be wrong. He could just be really, really into his coffee.

She went with honesty and hoped for the best. "I'm not a pack wolf."

He looked her way, and a flash of something—guilt? worry?—danced across his face before he nodded. "Never took you for one, to be honest."

"And I don't ever want to be one."

This time, he cocked his head, a definite question on his face. "Then don't be one."

That took her aback. "But this is a pack cabin."

He nodded slowly, cautiously. As if she might run away at his answer. "It is, but I'm not part of their pack."

She took a deep breath, trying to recenter herself. To push through her fear. "Oh. I sort of assumed."

"How about we stop assuming?" He turned off the stove, smiling. Two cups of coffee in his hands as he headed for the little dining table. "Tell me about yourself, Beautiful."

So she sat and she took the warm cup he offered and she let him in. A little bit.

"I grew up in a cabin much like this one. It was even tucked away along a mountain range—the Rockies instead of the Brooks Range, though. It was just as small and simple." She tried to keep the disdain out of her voice, knowing this shouldn't bother her as much as it did. Knowing how her disgust made her sound. But it was hard. That hatred ran deep, the sense of worthlessness a ragged scar that never quite healed properly. Still, she was more than that cabin in the Rockies. Always had been, always would be. And she shouldn't still feel the need to prove that.

"My parents left their pack when I was eight, though, and we traveled a lot."

"Always moving around."

"Yeah, but it never felt that way. It was more like a lifelong adventure."

"And where are your parents now?"

She stared into her cup, seeing her mother's face looking back at her. Same eyes, same cheeks, same lips—mirror images, her father had called them once. The resemblance strong enough that she couldn't deny it. "They died just before I came into adulthood."

Alaska reached across the table, wrapping his hand around hers. "I'm sorry for your loss."

"Thanks. It's fine—I mean, it's not *fine*, but it's…in the past."

"Still hurts, though." He said the words as if he knew, as if he understood.

"Definitely. So what about you? Where are you from, Alaska?"

"A country no longer even in existence."

"Oh, cagey. Will you ever give me a straight answer?"

"Maybe. Depends on the question."

"Figures." She yawned, unable to hold it back. "Excuse me. It's been a long day already."

"Are you tired?" Alaska frowned when she shook her head. "Don't worry—I fully intend to sleep on the couch. Go ahead and take a nap in the bed if you'd like."

Zoe shook her head again, holding back a smile. Alaska was a gentleman. She didn't run into too many of those anymore. When she'd first seen the bed, she'd assumed they'd be in it together. But he offered it to her, gave her the option of sleeping alone in it to make sure she was comfortable. He may have growled at Charlie's blatant ogling and propositioning, but he wasn't going to put her in an awkward position like making her share a bed with someone she barely knew.

His sweetness only made her want to jump his bones even more.

His intuitiveness made her wary, though.

"You look like a woman who wants to make herself comfortable but isn't." He stood before she could reply, heading for the small space by the door. "I'll tell you what. I'm going out for a run. You can either shift and join me—" his grin turned cocky as he stripped off his sweater and the white undershirt he wore "—or you can stay here and nap… or not nap. Whatever you want. I'll be back in time to make us dinner."

And then he dropped his pants.

Dropped. His. Pants.

Naked, gorgeous, flawless, the man stood before her completely comfortable without clothes on. With good reason. Corded with muscle, his arms hung relaxed at his sides, past his solid chest and waist, his hands brushing against his thick thighs. And cock. Definitely a thick cock. By the fates, there was a joke about the size of the state of Alaska versus his personal state of Alaska brewing in her head, but the fact that her mate stood naked before her for the first time was no joking matter.

"I have a feeling if I got naked right now to shift, there would be no running." She could have sworn his cock twitched at her words.

"I love the way you're staring at my cock, Beautiful," Alaska rumbled, though he contradicted the clear desire in his expression by taking a step away from her. Heading for the door. "Me, run. You, rest."

"Me, do whatever the fuck I want."

"Or that." Alaska chuckled and reached for the door. "See you in a few. Try not to think about me and my cock too much."

Too late. She was already imagining exactly what she could do with a cock like that, how well it would fill her. How she'd lick the tip and try to swallow it down. But he and his huge cock were already gone, the only sound the door closing behind him.

She was alone.

"As if I'd sit here and do nothing but think about you." Zoe rose to her feet and paced, trying hard to focus on anything other than the way her skin felt too tight, how slick she'd grown between her thighs. How needy she felt without Alaska nearby. With Alaska nearby. All the damn time, it seemed.

She lasted all of ten minutes.

"This won't end well," she told herself even as she stripped out of her clothes. And it definitely wouldn't end well at all—her wolf would take over once she saw her mate in his animal form, and there would be no stopping them from... well, mating. Fucking. Screwing. Doing the horizontal mambo. Enjoying a little amorous congress. Locking legs and swapping gravy.

"Stop thinking," she told herself, but she couldn't. The decision before her could change everything about her world. Could lead to her being joined to another shifter forever. Could be the best or worst thing that had ever happened to her. Could lead to the best sex of her life, too.

If she stepped out that door and shifted, she'd be getting laid before the evening was over. And possibly more than that—possibly mated. She knew better than to rush into that without some heavy thought. Knew that, if he got his teeth in her or she got hers in him, they'd be linked forever. Something she wasn't ready for.

Something she'd always considered a trap, one she'd sworn never to allow herself to fall into. But with Alaska, nothing felt confining. Not yet, at least. Maybe not ever? How could she know? She couldn't…and deep down inside, she knew she didn't need to.

Without thought or conscious decision, Zoe stepped outside, heading for the woods before the door even closed behind her. Taking a giant fucking leap of faith with every inch forward.

Her wolf practically howled in delight, ready to hunt down their mate. Ready to give herself to him.

And, the fates protect her, so was Zoe.

So she shifted forms, allowing her wolf control of their combined futures. Giving her the reins and letting their instincts take over. She caught the scent trail Alaska had left behind easily enough.

And she ran after him.

Nine

Deus paced in his wolf form not far from the cabin, guilt heavy on his shoulders. He'd lied to his mate—not directly, but by omission. For some reason, Beautiful seemed to have an absolute aversion to anything to do with pack wolves, he could sense it from her. So when she'd brought up his own situation, he'd answered her...in a roundabout fashion.

Why he couldn't just tell her about him, Luc, and his Dire Wolf pack, he didn't know. Perhaps it was the fact that he didn't trust her not to bolt just yet. Or that he was afraid she'd never want to be with him if she knew he was technically a pack wolf, no matter how untraditional his pack tended to be. He wanted her tied to him, wanted them to share everything, which meant he needed to be honest. But he needed to gain a little confidence first, to find the surety that he could keep her if he was.

He felt like a coward.

His wolf agreed with that assessment.

The thump of the cabin door closing caught his attention though, and suddenly his deceit was the furthest thing from his shared mind.

His mate was coming.

He could feel her presence, sense the ancient magic of her shifting from one form to another. He wanted to go to her, to hunt her down like prey, but something inside of him held him back. Some long-lost knowledge—almost an instinct—that told him to wait. To let her come to him. His beautiful girl didn't want to be chased.

She wanted to be the one to do the chasing.

So he ran farther into the woods.

Trees flew by as his paws pounded into the snow, the far-off peaks of the mountains visible along the skyline. Gorgeous territory this far north, but he preferred his city with all its noise and grit. Still, to be able to run this race, to allow his wolf to be free so his mate could hunt him down, almost felt like a gift. One that felt as if they could only share it right where they were—deep in the wilderness of Alaska. There was a reason Luc had called him up here, another why Deus had chosen to reach out to Beautiful the way he did. Fate had screamed in his ear and given him the chance at a life he hadn't thought possible anymore. No way would he stop listening to her now when he was so close to the finish line.

When he found a small clearing with fresh snow, he slid to a stop, unable not to take a moment and simply absorb the world around him. The trees hugged the edges of the open space, throwing shadows and making the snow turn an almost blue color. The mountains behind them rose up tall and wide as they blocked out part of the sky. Silence reigned, broken only by the harsh sounds Deus released as he stood there panting, his wolf completely focused on the trail he'd left. Waiting for his mate. Anxious to see her come through the trees. Running and chasing were fun, but Deus had a feeling being caught would be even better.

He could hear her before he could see her, practically

taste her scent on the wind as she barreled into the clearing and came to a stop.

And then he could only stare, a low growl rumbling automatically from his chest.

Stunning wasn't a big enough word. Small and lean, her wolf possessed a nearly silver coat that practically glittered in the fading sunlight. Bright eyes stared back at him. She held her head high, staring him down. Letting him know she wouldn't be weak. Her ears had jerked straight up, her tail trailing behind her. Strong, regal, amazing. She wouldn't bow to him in any sense of the word even if she was so much smaller than him. He would go so far as to call her dainty, though not to her face.

Beautiful crept closer, keeping her head up and her eyes locked on him. Not backing down for a single second. And though his wolf's growl turned harsher, though the animal inside of him made sure to let her know she was pushing him too far, the man inside the beast respected her pluck. She wouldn't allow him to tame her, so he'd have to be just as wild as she was.

Challenge accepted.

He stood stock-still as his mate reached him, as she sniffed all around him. Practically trembling as she slowly, cautiously rubbed her body against his. Whining softly, she nipped at the sensitive places around his neck and ears. The ones she could reach. She must have felt more comfortable as he stood so stiff because she worked her way farther back, laying her scent all over him.

Not moving seemed near impossible, but he fought through the need to respond to her. Battled his instincts to answer her obvious need, her ultimate canine affection. Like the powerful wolf he was, he held his ground. His wolf wanted to roll her over and bite down on her neck, to claim her as his with his teeth and her blood. The man in him wanted to shift, for her to shift as well, so he could run his human hands over her skin. To feel her.

Instead, when she finished covering him in her scent and sat before him as if expecting something, he did the only thing that felt right to the beast he truly was. He howled. Long and loud and soulful, he sang to the ancient moon and the spirits in the woods. To the fates that had given him the gift of such a female to be his. He called out to his brethren in the only way he knew.

Beautiful eventually joined him in his song, her head thrown back, her wolf howling to the sky above. Singing to the moon as their kind had done for thousands of years. Both voices coming together as one.

Deus had never felt so complete as he did in that moment. So utterly at home with another being beside him. And yet, he wanted more. Wanted to touch, to feel. To tease her, to witness her release, to taste it. He wanted the full mating experience, even if she wasn't ready to exchange bites. Even if she wasn't prepared to accept his essence yet or give him hers. He still wanted, and he wasn't going to wait any longer to take. So he shifted human, barely even noticing the slight chill around him. His desire burning bright enough to keep them both warm. With his eyes locked on hers, he sat back on his knees. Cock hard and jutting upward, eyes focused completely on her.

Offering himself to her.

Demanding nothing. Hoping for it all.

But he knew, if they were going to do this, do anything, it would have to be her decision.

He could only hope she made the one that would join them. Forever.

Ten

Zoe's wolf growled, the sound one of want and desire. Alaska—her fated mate—knelt a mere ten feet away, naked and calm. His hard cock pointed straight up into the air, a bead of precome glistening at the tip. The man looking so damned delicious, he made her crave him. Her mouth even watered at the very idea of getting a taste of him. She wanted…desperately.

She bared her teeth, though, digging her claws into the hard-packed ground. Her wolf wanted to mate—to join herself with the man before her. To sink her teeth into his neck and feel the mating pull completed. But human Zoe wasn't as sure.

"It's just me, Beautiful." Alaska held a hand out, reaching for her. Enticing her. She felt the pull to him, the draw of their bond. It bruised her body from the inside, making her joints hurt. Making everything ache. Every instinct wanted her to give in. Every experience of her life wanted her to hold back.

Instincts won that particular battle.

Zoe took two steps forward, shaking with the need building inside of her. Trembling from it. She wanted his body, his touch, and his kiss—wanted them so much, they were all she could think about. But she didn't want his bite. Not yet. And that…if she gave in to the desire, if she took what she wanted from him, the bite would follow. It had to. What wolf could resist the urge to complete a mating, the need to sink their teeth in deep during sex? No one. Especially not her.

Indecision pulled her up quick. She couldn't move another step. Couldn't decide whether it would be best just to give in or to keep fighting what she was beginning to see as the inevitable. She could still feel him against her skin, his wolf and hers rubbing alongside each other. Could still feel the tingles physical contact with her mate had caused. His touch had been electric. She wanted more. Of him, of them together, of this…just not everything.

"I won't hurt you," Alaska said, sitting back on his heels as he waited for her to do something. Anything. So very calm, her mate. She didn't want him calm—she wanted him grunting and grinding and falling apart at her touch. She wanted to feel him come inside her, to live with that overly wet, bruised feeling for the rest of the day, knowing it was because they'd been together.

By the fates, how she *wanted*.

Alaska sat still and calm, watching her, until watching must have become too much to deal with. His hand slid down his naked chest and over his rippled stomach. Heading south, heading to that long, hard piece of flesh she knew would bring her so much pleasure. Zoe couldn't look away. Couldn't stop staring as his fingers wrapped around the purple head and twisted before his fist slid down to the base. So fucking thick, this guy. So fucking gorgeous.

"I can feel how much you want this. How much you need to get off," Alaska said as he gave himself another slow stroke. "I can practically see the arousal pouring off of you. Stop fighting your instincts. Come. Take from me, Beautiful. Whatever we do today doesn't have to involve a mating bite. We can just fuck. You and me, right here under the sky. I'll fill you up nice and hard and deep. I'll even let you ride me so you can control what we do. I'm man *and wolf* enough to give that to you because I know you want it. You need that, don't you? The control. Well, it's yours. Every inch of me is yours, every bit of control too. I surrender, Beautiful. Just get over here and let me sneak a taste of that pussy, sweet girl. I'm so hungry for you."

She whimpered, the sound drawing a low rumble from his chest. She didn't have to bite him. In fact, she knew she wouldn't. Knew he'd keep his promise not to bite her, too. But she could mate with him, get off with him. Fuck him.

They were alone in Alaska for a reason, and one of those reasons could be to find out if they were compatible. Sex was an important component of that. She could give herself to him for a few nights, take what she wanted while she determined if they could move forward. It would be hard— so hard—if she decided to leave and not go through with the mating bites, but the plan seemed the safest. No surprises. No commitment before she felt ready. No trouble brewing on the horizon. Just her and Alaska and the passion they both felt for one another.

At least, that's what she told herself. Deep down, she knew once she crossed that line, there would be no coming back. Once they joined physically, they'd be connected. Not completely, he wouldn't be able to track her or sense her feelings, but there would always be a bond between them.

But maybe he'd be worth it.

So she shifted, and she dove for him, rolling through the

snow until she had pushed him to his back and landed on top of his hips. Even in human form, her growl shook through her as she pinned him down. Her wolf still so very close to the surface of her mind. Liking the dominance of the act, loving his submission.

Alaska smiled up at her, a look of wonder on his face as he reached to tuck her hair behind her ears. "I gave you the right nickname, Beautiful. You're so fucking stunning, as a wolf and a human."

And then he grabbed her neck and pulled her down, his lips overtaking hers. Hot and strong, he kissed with the force of his beast. Lapping into her mouth and dominating her tongue. His growl rumbled through the kiss, a possessive sort of sound that sent vibrations all the way down to her clit. Throbbing. She was absolutely throbbing for him.

"Get up here, Beautiful," Alaska said when he broke the kiss, adjusting his hips so his cock sat nestled in her slit. So he could tease her with every breath. "I want to feel you come on me."

"You think you can make me?"

His cocky grin nearly undid her. "Baby, I'll have you begging."

"I don't beg." But she had a feeling his bravado was based on more than attitude. Or maybe she just hoped, because being with a man good enough to make her beg for more sounded like a fine way to pass the time.

Alaska didn't answer her; he let his body do that talking. Rocking slow against her, he held her gaze as he began his patient torture. Every small thrust up had his cock hitting her clit, had her seeing stars and pushing closer to that edge. He kept his hands on her, sliding all over. Rubbing, teasing, worshiping with every inch of his big body. But it was the fire burning behind those icy green eyes that almost did her in. He wanted her, and nothing felt better than being desired by a man like him.

Not willing to give up the warmth of his touch just yet, wanting so much more of it, she slipped back off his hips and laid her body along his. The cold of the air around them kissed her skin, but she didn't mind it. Especially not as Alaska's hands worked their way down to her ass, holding her as he kneaded her flesh, spreading her cheeks with every hard grab. Rough but not too rough, strong but not overpowering. The perfect balance of taking what he wanted and letting her lead the way.

And Zoe loved it.

She planted a kiss on his soft lips, slicking her way inside for a taste. But she wanted the taste of more than his mouth. So she slid down his body, kissing and nibbling on his neck as he groaned and shook. To his chest, where she lapped over his flat nipples and earned a deep growl from him. She tasted every muscle along his abs, kissed and ran her fingers over every dip and ridge. And when she made it to his hips, when her chin brushed over the end of his cock, she teased him even more. Licking his hip bones, tickling along the V muscle she'd never know the name of but that made her stupid with desire. Rubbing her cheek along the length of his cock as if scenting him.

"Fuck, Beautiful. You're killing me here."

She grinned up at him, resting the side of her face against his cock and running a single finger down the length. "You ready to beg me to put my mouth on you yet?"

He laughed, muscles bunching, smiling bright. "You are a tricky one, aren't you?"

She chuckled with him before running her fingertips from hip bones to the base of his cock then up the length. Feeling a deep pang as he sucked in a breath, as his cock twitched in her hand. He was ready for more, and so was she.

Keeping her eyes on his, she rose up and licked the tip, tasting the salty precome there. Nearly giddy at the fire burning in his eyes. Unable not to tease him a little bit more. "So are you going to beg?"

"Fuck yeah, I'll beg." He curled up as she licked him again, his abs flexed and hard. Watching her with those icy eyes. Looking so damn hungry, it hurt. "Suck me, Beautiful. Take me deep. I'm fucking begging for your mouth on me. I've been dreaming of those thick lips wrapped around my cock since I met you."

Zoe had never been a girl to back down from a challenge. She also wasn't one to go slow. She gave Alaska a wink before opening her lips and sliding his cock between them. Deeper, more, sucking, licking, taking him in. Not giving him a break from the experience of being inside her mouth. Not letting up until she had him nudging the back of her throat.

Alaska fell back, groaning, arching his back as he begged for more. As he trembled under her touch. Zoe kept at it, kept pushing him harder. Kept sucking him. His hands shook as he dug his fingers into the snow, and his thighs sat tensed underneath her. Ready to let go already, fighting the urge to come. She loved watching him battle against his pleasure—against what she gave him—this strong, talented man at her mercy.

When she groaned with him still deep in her mouth, he grabbed her head. Tangled his fingers in her hair. Tugging, gently holding her down, keeping her on him as he rocked just enough to fuck her mouth. To take what he needed while still not demanding. She could have pulled away, could have backed off him even with his hands on her, but she wouldn't. Didn't want to. What she wanted was to keep sucking him. To drive him wild. To make him come.

Her pussy clenched on nothing, soaking wet and so ready to be filled. But not yet. It was his turn, and if he was going to make her beg, she'd damn well make sure he did it first. More than just with words. She wanted his body begging for hers. So she sucked hard, groaning again the way she already knew he liked. Swallowing around him as he jolted beneath her.

"Your mouth is a fucking dream. Look at you take all of me." He pressed deeper, staring down at her, looking like a beast ready to explode. And then he bit his lip, pushing deeper into her throat, and she damn near whimpered at how hot that expression on his face made her. "Too much?"

She pulled all the way to the tip and sank back down, proving how *not too much* this was. Alaska kept his hands in her hair, guiding, not pushing but definitely controlling. Growing more harried with every move, more needful and lost to his pleasure. So hot, her mate. So sexy as he took his pleasure.

Unable to stop herself, needing to find her own release, she straddled his leg and rubbed her pussy against his thigh. Rocking her hips back and forth to find some sort of release from the need burning through her.

"Is that your cunt so wet against my leg?" He shook his head when she sucked him harder in response. "Damn, Beautiful. You're a needy thing, aren't you? Responsive as fuck to your mate."

He reached down and tweaked her nipple, making her jump. Making her roll her hips harder over his muscles. She was going to come. Not from his mouth or his fingers or even the cock in her mouth. She was going to come because of his fucking thigh gliding along her clit. And she had a feeling she was going to love it.

But Alaska apparently had other plans. "You're so wet. I can't waste that."

He jackknifed up, grabbing her by the waist and

pulling her off him before spinning her around. She ended up lying across his body, his cock in her face, but this time—

"Turnabout's fair play, and I always like to be fair." Alaska licked her. Licked her pussy from opening to clit. One long, slow, torturous motion that had her gasping and arching and shoving her hips back for more. Focusing on her own pleasure and neglecting his. He smacked her ass for that one, rubbing away the sting right after. "Get back to work, woman."

And then he attacked her clit with that wicked tongue. Zoe groaned and rubbed against him, the need building. Distracted but not wanting to tap out and simply enjoy the way he ate her, she sucked him back into her mouth. The angle wrong to take him as deep as before. Still, the two worked in tandem, both groaning and moaning and rocking and losing control. Zoe kept his cock wet and hard, licking and sucking and swallowing around him. And Alaska…well, Alaska had a lot of hidden talents. He used his thumbs to keep her lips spread, and he suckled her clit without mercy. Lashing it with his tongue whenever he broke contact. Never letting up. Never giving her a break from the assault.

Zoe's orgasm hit her just as Alaska pressed two big, thick fingers inside her. Her entire body locked down, the world freezing for a split second before she exploded, spinning out of control in her own mind as pleasure rocked through her. Alaska grunted underneath her, thrusting up into her mouth three times before coming. Before cursing and arching and filling her throat.

Both growling.

Both sated.

For the moment.

Alaska groaned after he'd caught his breath, running his hands over her shoulders and back. "While I'll never turn down a chance to get your mouth on my cock or to eat this sweet pussy, next time, I want to do it where there aren't spruce branches poking me in the ass."

She laughed and moved to turn around, lying along the length of him again. "Some guys might like being poked in the ass while getting their cock sucked."

He growled and yanked her up until she practically straddled his chest, his eyes brighter than normal. His wolf so very close to the forefront of his mind that the very sight called to hers.

"We can explore ass-poking later, preferably with me doing the poking to that phenomenal ass of yours. Right now, though, I want you sitting on my face. I want you to fucking soak me, and then I want to get that cunt good and sloppy again."

Oh, his dirty, dirty mouth would be the death of her. "Well, aren't you sweet."

He rolled her over, growling. Dropping a soft, heartbreaking kiss to her lips. Keeping it slow but deep, giving her the freedom to break away. Not that she'd want to.

And when he finally pulled back, he kept his hand in her hair as he stared down at her. The amazed expression back on his face. "You're the most gorgeous woman I've ever seen. Beautiful is too generic for you, too boring. Every inch of you is a masterpiece, the entire package a work of art. I am honored that you allowed me the privilege of tasting your release. Watching you come, capturing all that sweetness on my tongue, was a gift. One I'd never take advantage of." He ran a thumb over her cheek and smiled, tugging at her heartstrings. Warming her heart and her body. But the cocky glint returned to his eyes, his lips curing into an almost-arrogant smirk as he said, "I can't resist touching your soft skin, but if I don't bury myself balls deep in your wet, soft pussy soon, I might go mad."

So damn charming. She laughed, biting her lip to keep from shooting him a goofy grin. "We can't have that."

"Exactly." He rolled them over and swatted her ass. "Get up, woman. We've got a run back to the cabin, and then I'm fucking that pussy until you come at least three more times."

She always had loved a man with a plan.

Eleven

Deus raced after his mate's silver wolf, dodging trees and growling the entire way back to the cabin. They weren't in a fun run or a jaunt through the woods. They ran with purpose, with determination and a goal. They were running home to have sex. Lots and lots of sex. Fated mate sex.

He didn't quite know how to process that.

Twelve hundred years. That was an exceptional amount of time to exist without a mate by your side. He'd long ago given up hope he'd ever meet his. Even after his Dire brothers started finding their females and falling into matings one by one, he'd assumed his would simply never appear. He and Luc—the bachelors of the group. He would have been okay with that.

He would *not* be okay with it now that he'd met Beautiful.

Fuck, he still didn't know her name, though she'd forever be Beautiful to him. He wasn't kidding when he'd said the word was too generic for her, though. There was no descriptor for how gorgeous she was. Nothing in the seventeen languages he spoke to accurately describe how she stole his breath every time she looked his way with those wide, hazel eyes. He'd been gifted a dream, a woman who stunned him stupid simply by existing and who had a wickedly smart head on her shoulders. He couldn't ask for anything more.

But as his mate reached their little cabin in the woods and shifted human, as she stood naked before him, a teasing smile on her face as she wagged a finger for him to come closer, he knew that was a lie. He *could* ask for more—more time, more skin, more touch, more of being with her. That was the more he'd happily request every day for the rest of his life. He'd flown to Alaska to deal with Luc and his needs, but right then, with the sun setting and the chill settling into the area, work was as far from his mind as it ever had been. He had a gorgeous woman with him, one the fates deemed his perfect match. One who seemed to want him as much as he wanted her. And nothing would get in the way of him enjoying her body for at least a few hours.

So he shifted human, and he obeyed her demand to follow her until he stood close enough to feel her breath on his chest. To sense her need for him to fill the silence. Something he could and would do for her.

"You wanted me, Beautiful?"

Her hands skated over his chest and up around his shoulders, her eyes following as if amazed he stood before her. "Not past tense. *Want.* I want you, Alaska."

Alaska, not Deus. Fuck, if she ever said his real name, he'd come. Right there, didn't matter, no touches required—he'd come like a pup having his first wet dream. Instead, he growled and picked her up, his hands squeezing her ass tight as he carried her through the open door.

"I promised to fuck you," Deus said, his voice far too deep and rough. Couldn't help it—the woman made him an animal even in his human form.

"After you let me ride your face."

"Beautiful, there's no letting. I'm yours. Take what you want. All of it will be a gift to me."

She looked so shocked, so surprised that he could want to fuck her through the floor and also let her use him for her pleasure. And he did...both. He had no problem giving up his control to her. In fact, he was pretty damn sure he'd enjoy every second of it.

"You're too good to be real," she whispered, as if he wouldn't hear her. But he did, and he felt the same way about her.

"I'm real. I promise you that. Let me take care of you," he replied, pulling her tighter against him and moving them toward the bed. "Whatever you want. Whatever you need. Give me the chance to be the one to make sure you have it."

Deus was too far gone to know if he meant sex or love or life or a mix of all three, but he didn't care. He'd give her the world if she let him. So he laid her down, and he crawled back between her legs. Slow caresses up and down her thighs led to her groaning and twisting, searching for more. Small licks of her pussy led to her hands in his hair, pulling and yanking him closer. Fighting for her first orgasm since they made it back to the cabin. And her second. And, with her finally sitting on his face and riding his tongue like a goddamned jockey, her third.

His cock ached, his hips thrusting of their own volition as he sought some form of release. As he listened to her come over and over again with her taste on his tongue and her scent surrounding him. So when she spun off him, falling onto her back on the mattress, he took advantage of the opportunity to roll on top of her. To settle between her welcoming thighs. To smile down at the woman the fates deemed his perfect match and get lost in the soft, sexy expression there.

"I'll show you," he whispered as he nudged his way inside. "I'll prove to you I'm a good mate."

She didn't reply, simply held his gaze as she wrapped her

legs around his hips and tugged him deeper. And fuck, was she soft. Soft and wet and so damn hot inside. He had to count in his head to keep from coming before he was all the way in. Had to focus on anything other than the feel of her to be able to move. He'd wanted to fuck her slowly, to drag his cock in and out without hurry, but she felt too good. Too swollen and welcoming. He couldn't resist another second.

"Beautiful," he groaned, dropping his head to her shoulder and trying hard not to buck his hips.

"Do it, Alaska. Fuck me. Doesn't matter how. I want to feel you come. I need to see it."

Best mate ever. He let go of his leash, thrusting hard, sliding in balls deep before pulling back out and doing it again. Beautiful groaned and hissed, clawing at his shoulders, rocking her hips in tandem with his until they were mindless, unstoppable sex machines moving together toward a similar goal. Toward completion.

Fuck, his wolf wanted to bite her.

His teeth lengthened, his mouth watering as he stared at her neck. His wolf wanted to claim their mate, to link themselves forever together. But he'd promised, so he held the beast back. Suffering from it, but not breaking his word to her. He couldn't. They already had so much crap between them, so many diversions and slight untruths, they didn't need something like a shattered promise to add to the pile.

But when she arched and threw her head back as she came, as her pussy clenched all around his thick cock, the temptation became too much. Way too much. His wolf shoved to the front of his mind and demanded they bite. They sink their teeth into the flesh they saw as *theirs*. Into the mate gifted to them, to claim her forever. He couldn't stop himself, couldn't feel the pulse of her pussy on him and not react to it. Couldn't—

With power only being paired to a beast for so long

could bring, Deus yanked the wolf back into his mental cage. It wasn't enough, though. His teeth were too long, his mouth too wet. His need to bite too strong. And her neck was *right there*. But he'd promised her...he'd told her they could just have sex. He couldn't let his mate down.

Groaning, focusing hard on every muscle movement required just to get through the process, Deus pulled out of the heaven that was Beautiful's pussy. Without pause, he flipped her to her side, straddled one of her legs from behind her, and slid back inside. Pounding home, using the intensity of the workout to distract himself from everything else he wanted. From the desire pulsing through him to join them in a more permanent way. Exhausting his muscles to make the temptation go away.

Beautiful took his roughness all in stride, reaching back to grab his hip as he shoved his way inside her over and over again. Making these delicious, breathy sounds on every push. Sounds that torqued his need to come higher. And when it was his turn to fall over that edge, to feel the burn of his orgasm start in his lower belly and explode throughout the rest of his body, she dug her claws into his hip hard and pulled him tight. Not a bite but the pain felt close enough to one to settle his wolf even if only for the moment. To give him a taste of what he truly wanted.

"Mine." He collapsed on top of her with his face buried in her neck, breathing hard. Scenting her. Her body stiffened, though. It didn't take him but a second to figure out why—their position, his mouth so close to her neck, his breath on her skin. Yeah, he knew. Deus chuckled and ran a hand over her hip as he slid backward a few inches, just enough to move his mouth to her shoulder instead of her neck. "Relax, baby. I'm not going to bite you. I know you're not ready for all the claiming stuff, and I'm upholding my promise. But right now?" Deus slid a hand over her hip to cup her sweet cunt. "This pussy is mine. My wolf says so, and the human side of me agrees. And we promise to take real good care of it."

Beautiful relaxed into his hold, even rubbing against his fingers a little. Teasing herself. "If you take any better care of it than you already have, I might not walk for a week."

"I see nothing wrong with that." He laughed as she swatted at him, rolling her over and wrapping himself around her. As he pinned her down. As he nearly lost all control at the smile on her pretty face. Those lips would be the death of him. "You and me, Beautiful. For a few days, a week, a year, forever. We'll work out the details. But for right now? Let's just be us. Together."

She nodded, and he leaned down to kiss her irresistible lips. To take advantage of their position and enjoy his access to her a little longer. The fates only knew how long he'd have her. He wanted forever, but he had a feeling he was going to have to fight her to get it.

He would, though.

He'd fight the whole goddamned world for her.

Twelve

Zoe came awake slowly, achy and sore but satisfied. For the most part, at least. Her wolf still had desires they hadn't touched on. The beast loved the physicality of her mate, though. She was a tactile creature, and that craving had transferred to Zoe. Both of them liked to be touched by the people or wolves they trusted. Loved the feel of another's skin against hers, their weight on her. Apparently, Alaska had been added at some point to that list of approved touches. Otherwise, she'd be panicking.

Alaska had her wrapped in his arms, his breath on her neck and his hard body almost covering hers. Most people might have felt stifled or uncomfortable, but she didn't. No, instead, she only felt safe. Protected. Hell, if she was being honest with herself, she felt cared for. And wasn't that the scariest thing ever? At least in the theory that she could come to expect it. To rely on his attention. If he left her? If he got careless with her as men tended to do? If she became accustomed to him being so sweet and kind and attentive, then she lost that? It could break her.

Her wolf issued a low growl inside her head, not liking the thought of being afraid of their mate. Of him leaving her or letting her down. The old animal remembered the past but didn't dwell on it the way human Zoe did. She was more forgiving, her instincts telling her to trust her mate. To give herself over to him. Human Zoe wasn't there yet.

Alaska moved, drawing her closer as if he'd heard her thoughts. As if he'd understood them and was trying to calm her frazzled nerves. His heavy thigh pushed between hers, his thick cock trapped between his stomach and her ass. The man was just so big and strong—not her usual type at all, but still the sexiest male she'd ever seen.

That might have been her wolf's opinion, though.

He moved again, sighing in his sleep, pulling her tighter as the thigh between her legs moved higher. Moved right up against her pussy. Already wet and swollen from the night before, her flesh responded to his contact, sending sparks of pleasure shooting up into her belly. She wanted him again. Wanted him badly.

But first, she wanted to make him squirm.

Carefully, intentionally trying not to wake him, she rolled over to face him. It took some maneuvering, what with him being a human blanket and all, but she made it. She even switched legs so he could keep his thigh pressed against where she was so hot for him already. She might have even rubbed against him a little. A girl had needs—ones she knew he'd happily take care of once she was done teasing him.

Biting her lip to keep from grinning, she dragged her hand down his arm and over his hip. He moved with her, almost undulating to follow the touch. Zoe could have done that all day, watching his muscles bunch and flex as she touched him, but she had other plans. Places she wanted to touch that were far more interesting than his arm.

So she slipped her hand between them, and she wrapped her fingers around his cock. And she stroked him slow and hard with her hand squeezing him tight. Alaska growled and whined, rocking his hips into her hold, his forehead furrowing and his lips parting as he groaned. And when his eyes opened, when that ice green suddenly appeared and blazed as he took her in, Zoe finally grinned.

"Morning, handsome." She ran her thumb over the tip of his cock before stroking faster, tugging and twisting his hard flesh.

Alaska kept thrusting into her hand, lifting his leg to press his thigh tighter against her pussy and groaning. "Fuck me, Beautiful. This is one hell of a wake-up call."

"I'd have used my mouth, but you almost had me trapped underneath you."

He growled again, longer this time. Louder. "I like you being underneath me."

He proved his statement by pulling her hand away from his cock and rolling them over, spreading her wide as he nudged his way inside. As he stretched her tender flesh and made her shake with the need for more and harder and faster.

"Perfect fucking cunt," he whispered, almost as if he didn't want her to hear it. As if he didn't expect to say those words out loud. Zoe dug her nails into his back and prodded his ass with her heel, groaning when he bucked harder. Sighing when he finally gave her what she wanted. A thick cock pounding inside of her as her sexy beast of a man lost control on top of her. Every thrust pushed deeper, every move so rough she had to grunt and whine to release the tension they caused. And she loved it. Loved every second of it.

"Want you to come," she murmured in his ear, biting the fleshy lobe before practically purring. "Want to feel you dripping out of me all morning."

"Ah, fuck, Beautiful." Alaska jerked harder, snapping his hips and dragging her up the bed. With a growl, he grabbed her hips and flipped her over, spreading her legs and pushing her shoulders to the mattress. Ass up…doggy style. Fitting, really. And when he slammed back home, when he fucked his way inside her and hit places she hadn't even known existed as he bottomed out, she exploded.

Shaking, keening, falling apart as he took from her, she came on his cock with her face buried in the mattress and her hands fisting the sheets. And it was good. Better than good. Pleasure rocked every inch of her, moving like a wave from her core to her neck and back down to her toes. Even her fingers tingled.

And when Alaska came, when he roared and pressed deep, holding still for a good ten seconds before rocking those last few times, she got her wish. Even with him still inside her, his come dripped down her thighs. The perfect way to start their first full day in Alaska—and Alaska's first full day inside of her.

"Fuck." Alaska fell onto the mattress, making the whole bed shake. Zoe grunted her agreement and dropped next to him, curling into his hold once more. Her head on his chest, her hands on his stomach. Her pussy tingling from his assault. "Best wake-up call ever."

She grinned, unable not to. "So what's for breakfast?"

He huffed a laugh and tugged her closer. "Give me about ten minutes, and I'll happily have my breakfast between those thighs of yours."

"That's awfully one-sided. What am I going to eat?"

His lips kicked up in a cocky sort of smile. "That's why I need the ten minutes. We can have a repeat of yesterday in the woods."

She groaned and inched closer. "That was a lot of fun."

"Definitely."

But their happy bubble didn't last—not two minutes later, his phone pinged. And then pinged again. Five times. Eight. Alaska groaned and rolled, keeping his hand on her tit as he looked at the ceiling.

"You going to get those?"

"They mean work." He turned his head to catch her eye, a frown marring that handsome face. "They'll mean I have things to do outside of this bed."

She shrugged. "So we'll do it together, and then we can come back here and do *things* together inside this bed again. And maybe the kitchen. The shower has possibilities."

He growled and rolled, landing on top of her and placing a huge, wet kiss to her lips. Tongues sliding, they gripped and tugged and rubbed against one another. Teasing. Knowing they couldn't finish what they wanted to. Not yet, at least.

Deus broke the kiss first. "You're such a naughty girl."

"You already knew this about me."

"I did." He teased the tip of his cock through her slick folds, making her gasp his name. Making her need. "What I didn't know was how my little deviant cat burglar had a pussy that would make me lose my mind."

She grinned and bit his lip as he came in for another kiss, releasing him when he moaned deeply. "Work, remember?"

"Fuck." He held still, breathing hard, cock right at her entrance. Body so damn stiff as he held himself over her. As he resisted the urge to slide right inside her. "This is going to be the longest day ever."

She ran her hands over his back, agreeing but also looking forward to teasing him. "Maybe we'll find a closet to hole up for a few minutes. Take a break from work to have a little fun someplace the humans won't notice."

He jerked back, eyes bright and face shocked. "Yeah?"

She nodded, running a single finger over his bicep. "I love the idea of having you come in my mouth in some dark, shadowy corner where we might get caught."

He stared, not moving. Not even breathing for a good thirty seconds. "Fuck me, the fates wanted to kill me. That's why they gave me you." He kissed her deeply again before bounding off the bed.

"Where are you going?" she asked with a laugh, rolling to watch that amazing ass as he crossed the room.

"Phone, breakfast, work. And if I get to come inside your mouth at some point during that time, I'll be a happy man." He dove back onto the bed, phone in hand, but looking right at her. "And if I get to lick up every drop of you when I suck on your clit and finger you until you come, I'll be damn near giddy."

"Giddy?"

"Motherfucking giddy. Now get up, sweet cheeks— you can shower first. Let me deal with these calls, and then I want to feed that fuckhot mouth of yours before we start our day."

Deus waited for his mate to run the shower before stepping outside. Wolf shifter hearing was too strong for true privacy, but the rumble of the water in such a confined space would blur out the majority of his conversation. At least, he hoped it would.

He also hoped he could keep this call short. The lure of all that naked flesh flushed and wet from the warm water called to him, but his responsibilities wouldn't let him partake. He needed to talk to Luc, to set up the plan for the next few days, and to make sure his Alpha didn't require more than Deus had prepared for.

He didn't even bother looking over the text messages or listening to the voice mails that had been left, choosing instead to call Luc right away. A good plan, as it seemed his Alpha's patience had run out.

"Where the fuck have you been?"

Deus flinched at the tone in Luc's voice, his wolf fighting the urge to submit to the more powerful beast on the other end of the call. "I'm in Alaska."

"I know that. You arrived yesterday with a woman. Something you want to tell me?"

Fuck. Double fuck. It wasn't that Deus didn't want to tell his Dire brothers about Beautiful, but he wasn't ready yet. Wasn't sure how things would go with this mating. For what was likely the first time in his very long life, he felt uncertain about a situation and absolutely refused to show such a weakness to his pack.

But he also wouldn't lie to Luc. "I've found my mate."

Luc's rough chuckle came as a surprise. "I know that too, Deus. I felt the pull when you were still in New York, though there's static in the bond. You haven't completed the mating yet."

"No. Not yet. She's…" *Stubborn, skittish, unnerving, independent, the most terrifying creature I've ever met* "uncomfortable with the idea of forming such a permanent bond with someone she doesn't know."

"So get to know her."

"I'm working on it."

Luc grunted, the sound telegraphing his doubt. "Speaking of work, I need you to get that intel."

"We're heading into town today to do some recon and start digging."

"We? You're taking her on the job with you?"

No way was he not. He simply couldn't fathom leaving her alone in an unknown location. "Definitely."

"Good. That works out even better than if you'd come alone."

"Why's that?"

"The pack is on edge—there's a negative energy around the area that seems to be fueling their unrest. You alone might stand out as a threat to them. You with your mate won't. You can go undercover as a couple on your Klunzad."

A trip shifters sometimes took after a mating to get away from everyone, allowing them to learn about one another. Sort of a shifter honeymoon. And a brilliant idea. "We can run with that plan."

"Good. But keep an eye on—what's your girl's name?"

Deus blinked, staring out into the forest as the sun topped the trees. A heavy weight settling on his chest. "I don't know, but I call her Beautiful."

Luc's silence spoke volumes. As did his incredulous tone as he asked, "Are you telling me you don't even know her name yet, but you brought her on a mission?"

It sounded so much worse when he put it that way. "I couldn't leave her in the city, and she has skills that might come in handy."

"What kind of skills?"

"She's a thief."

"A thief." Deadpan, flat…doubt-filled.

"A cat burglar, if you will."

"Is she a good one?"

Memories of her taking out those men who'd set up to scam her flashed through his mind, pictures of her sass and her confidence making him both hard as stone and proud. "She's fucking amazing."

"Then she may be an asset in this situation. Do what you need to do to get information on the pack and the area, but be subtle. I don't want to cause more unrest without understanding the situation."

"Roger that." Deus heard the shower turn off inside the cabin, a sure sign Beautiful would be able to hear him. Time to wrap things up. "Is there anything else?"

"Yeah. Congratulations. Try not to get too caught up in the mating haze."

The inability to focus on anything other than sex that often happened to newly mated couples. An event he'd never seen himself and doubted was anything more than desire boiling over. He had immense control—no way would such a thing be an issue for him and his mate. "Won't be a problem."

Again with the chuckle. "Sure. Right. Be careful out there, call me as soon as you know anything, and don't fuck this up."

Luc ended the call without specifying what *this* he meant—the job or the mating. Either way, Deus had a feeling both were far more precarious than he would have liked. But as he pocketed his phone and headed inside, his determination to succeed at them both only grew. Nothing as dubious as the supposed mating haze would stop him from getting his job done. And no way would he allow anything to come between him and his fated mate.

Only death would separate them now.

Thirteen

Having his beautiful mate's little hand in his as they walked through what would technically be called a town was something Deus hadn't expected to enjoy so much. There was something sweet about the moment, something that accentuated their connection. A simple gift of time and touch that implied togetherness. Having the scent of her cunt lingering on his skin didn't hurt either.

But the time to mate and taste and fuck all over the cabin had passed with the numerous messages and phone calls from Luc. Information was necessary, research had to happen, and the mission needed to be completed. Deus had a job to do—one that would require him to dig deep into the local histories and culture, the legends that likely grew from a spark of truth. One his Alpha wanted handled subtly. Deus couldn't storm in and demand.

The job for Luc and Deus' growing relationship with his mate seemed to be following similar tracks.

So Deus had enacted the plan Luc had recommended to

stay under the radar of the townspeople and local pack. One Beautiful was a vital part of. What made every single man seem less of a threat? A woman on his arm. Acting as a newly mated couple enjoying the solitude of the Alaskan wilderness and wandering through town as tourists seemed as good of a cover as any. And thankfully, they didn't have to act too hard. They were newly mated, and they were enjoying the solitude of the wilderness. He hoped they'd enjoy it more later that night.

Though having Beautiful at his side—walking with her through the grungy town—definitely defied the concept of subtle. His mate shone wherever she went, dressing like a million dollars and looking even more valuable. Beautiful didn't begin to describe her, ever. The cold had given a little extra color to her cheeks, which contrasted well with the winter-white coat she wore that covered what he knew was a soft, tight sweater and leather skirt. She'd lined her eyes in a smoky gray, making them appear even larger than normal. And those lips. Bright red, plump, and perfect—they called to him. Made him want to taste them every chance he got. Made him want to see them wrapped around his cock. He'd become obsessed with her and red. Who could blame him?

No one. "You look amazing, by the way. Did I tell you that?"

Those lips ticked up a bit. "Only about thirty times so far today."

"Expect me to tell you thirty more. You really are stunning, though I'm worried about those shoes."

Beautiful glanced down, frowning at her own feet. "What's wrong with my shoes?"

Nothing. High and sexy as fuck, the heels on her feet would look amazing up in the air as he buried his face between her legs, or digging into his ass as he fucked her against a wall. He loved those shoes. "This place isn't exactly made for walking. I worry you'll ruin them."

"Then I'll buy more."

"They seem expensive."

"They are."

"You could have worn something…less valuable and not had to worry about replacing them."

"What fun is that?" She grinned up at him, making his world pause for just a moment. "I like the finer things in life, Alaska. Why bother getting dressed at all if you can't be a little showy?"

He didn't argue with her, just smiled and brought her hand to his lips so he could kiss the back of it. "Next time we just won't get dressed at all."

Her hazel eyes practically glittered as she said, "Deal."

So they walked, and they held hands, and they stopped occasionally to kiss or touch a little more as Deus planned all the things he wanted to do to her body when they got back to the cabin. He also ran through all the ways he could find the information Luc needed.

Names.

Dates.

Crimes.

Population records.

Genealogy within the local pack.

How these shifters had lead such isolated lives for so long without attracting the attention of the humans around them.

All things he wouldn't find online, sadly. Only in this lonely, sequestered little town.

When his mate stopped to look in the window of a small storefront, Deus stood beside her. Watching her more than anything inside the store. Unable to look away. She had her hair pulled up, and her long neck appeared endlessly bitable.

A thought that refused to leave his mind. A need he couldn't shake no matter how many times he told himself that wouldn't be happening. Not yet at least. Especially not today.

Still, he couldn't look away.

"Do you sense them?" Beautiful asked, still not looking at him.

He hummed, wondering how deep he would need to sink his teeth into that flesh to mix his essence with hers. "Who, my sweet?"

"The other wolves." She turned, leaving the window behind and taking a step closer to the street. "We haven't run into any, but I can scent them under the more dominant human smells. They've been around."

That thought, the potential threat of running into an unfamiliar pack, refocused his priorities. And when his mate showed fear, when she shivered as if the thought of strangers instilled a sense of being unsafe, Deus growled. "I won't let them near you."

"I'm not worried about that," she said, though her tone betrayed her words. "It's more…I find it odd that humans and wolves live together like this. Small town, low population—I'd think the wolves would pick an area where they could hide more."

"They have the woods to hide in out here."

"True, but they come to town. This place reeks of them." She curled in on herself, frowning. "I feel as if we're being watched."

Deus let his senses spread, used sight and hearing and the scents on the air to evaluate the area. He didn't feel the same sort of under-the-microscope sensation that she did, but he did notice an anticipatory energy that scraped along his nerves. Something hovering over the area, something dark and wrong. One he couldn't tell her about as that knowledge would only exacerbate her fear.

It was a good time for a distraction.

He leaned against the lamppost and tugged her against him, wrapping his arms around her hips and nuzzling her neck. Holding her tight to both to get a feel of her and to keep her safe. "We're not local, and it's a small town. Of course, they're watching us. Meanwhile, I'm watching you. That skirt hugs your ass just right. Makes me want to bite it."

"You're obsessed."

"With my mate, yes? With that ass? Absolutely." Distraction—achieved. And yet, he felt the need to reassure her as well, so he leaned closer and lowered his voice. "I feel the others too. I'm not sure if they're watching or not, but they're close."

"What should we do?"

"Act normal. Keep pretending to be a newly mated couple on vacation." He caged her in tighter, dropping a kiss to her neck. "Find a quiet spot to slip my hands under that fuckhot leather and see if I can get you off before anyone notices what I'm doing. The skirt was a nice touch—easy access later."

"I *am* a girl with a plan." She groaned when he pressed his hard cock against her. When he nibbled lightly on her shoulder. Fuck, he loved that sound, especially when he had the taste of her skin on his tongue. When he could rub his body against hers. When he could grab her ass and slip his hand—

"Maybe we should keep walking." She tugged out of his hold, smiling up at him as if she knew how distracted she made him. And she did—her pink cheeks and her bright eyes told him she knew exactly what she was doing to him.

"Where do you want to go?"

"Anywhere. I want to see what this place has to offer other than all the beefcake."

"Beefcake?"

"You haven't noticed? There are no women here. It's all men. This part of Alaska is a veritable sausage fest."

He hadn't noticed, but he wasn't all that surprised. Alaska was known for having a much larger population of men than women. Though to have none in town...that seemed impossible. There had to be women around somewhere.

"There's a bank," Beautiful said suddenly, staring across the street at a small, squat building. "I don't even see a guard inside it."

His little cat burglar. "They probably only carry a few thousand dollars at a time in there."

She shrugged, completely casual—intentionally so—as her eyes darted over every inch of the building. "I was just looking. I mean, you *are* taking me away from my work back home. I could try to *steal* a little time away from you one night."

That wouldn't be happening. Still, he laughed at her little play on words, dragging her past the building that had snagged her attention so completely. "We're probably the only tourists in this town. I thought you didn't like to be obvious."

"You're such a spoilsport. A girl has needs, you know."

He did know. He'd gotten to know hers quite well. So he yanked her into his arms and kissed her, taking what he wanted from her. Demanding entrance and tangling his tongue with hers until she melted against him. Until he had her body all soft and pliant and ready for more. Then he pulled back.

"I know all about your needs, little mate. I think I've been pretty good about meeting them too."

She shot him a saucy grin. "Such a dirty wolf."

"Such a beautiful one."

And so their day went. They explored, looked around, secretly investigated, all the while cuddling and teasing and kissing. Deus asked the locals questions while Beautiful charmed them, both of them pretending to be excited to learn about the nowhere town they'd happened upon. He didn't finish his research for Luc, but he had a good start. One that he could build on once they hit the libraries and dug through cases of microfiche and old newspapers. Not his favorite things.

But the day wasn't a complete waste. He'd spent it with his mate instead of alone. He'd even gotten a bit of a foot job sitting in a corner booth at the only restaurant in town. Bonus, though he'd definitely make her finish that later. It'd been hot as fuck to sit there and have to be still as she ran her little foot all over his cock. Her wicked smirk had been far more obvious that she'd been up to something than any reaction Deus could have given. He wanted to play more of that game—see if he could get her to break. If she could still focus on her meal if he crawled beneath the table and spread her legs. Took a little taste of her. At least, that was where his mind was as they stepped out of the restaurant.

And ran smack into a big, obviously pissed-off wolf shifter.

"You're not welcome here," the man said, his voice more growl than not. His long hair lay unkempt against his shoulders, and the cloak he wore looked old and threadbare. Shifter—definitely shifter. How any human in the area could see him as one of their own, Deus didn't know. Doubted they could at all. This man was pure animal. He even reeked of the forest, a definite sense of wilderness lingering about him.

And his eyes refused to leave Deus' mate.

Something she noticed, if the way she stiffened up and took a step closer to Deus' side was any indication.

Deus couldn't throw the mission, though. Couldn't risk Luc by blowing their cover. So he kept Beautiful against him, kept his wolf chained up so he didn't attack the man for daring to even look at his mate. And he chose his words carefully. "We're just visiting—"

The man flipped his focus to Deus, that anger still boiling below the surface. "I don't give a fuck why you're here. *She's* not welcome."

The venom behind the words, the warning in them being directed at Beautiful caused Deus' wolf to bristle hard. Caused his brain to shift into instinct mode. Deus had nothing to say to the shifter—he had to actually bite his tongue, because he knew if he opened his mouth, he'd challenge the fucker to a battle. And though he had no problem fighting for this mate, he needed to think of Luc's directives. To stay subtle, avoid attention. Fly under the radar. Luc's work, this project, needed to stay as secretive as possible. Deus had to control himself too for the sake of the mission, though if the guy took one step toward Beautiful, the mission could go fuck itself.

Thankfully, the other man turned and stalked out into the street, leaving them alone. But not before looking over his shoulder at Beautiful one last time. "Leave here, or we'll drag you out ourselves."

Deus watched the man leave, staying in front of his mate. Standing sentry between her and the wild man. Protecting her. And when he turned, when he saw his mate's face, all that protectiveness flared hot and bright beneath his skin.

Scared. His mate looked scared.

"Beautiful?" The word came out as a growl, his wolf responding to her obvious discomfort. At the slight bit of fear and pain on her face. Ready to fight anyone who could make her feel that way and prove his strength.

But in mere seconds, her expression changed. All that fear—that anxiety—gone. Mask in place, she shrugged as if the entire experience had meant nothing to her. "I have no idea who that was, but apparently, I'm not welcome in this town."

"You're welcome wherever I am. I'll make sure of it."

Her lips turned up in a smile, one that came nowhere near touching her eyes. Deus knew a front when he saw one. He could almost taste the lies she would spin about this moment. How she'd pretend to be brave so he wouldn't point out a weakness. As if he'd even think of it.

So instead of pushing her, he lifted her hand to his mouth and kissed it. "I have your back if you want to kick his ass."

"As if I'd need help from a computer geek like you."

"You never know. These fingers could be deadly."

His mate laughed and tugged on his hand, leading him in the opposite direction of where the man had gone. Retreating for the moment. Deus went along willingly. This was her show, her moment. She'd been the one called out, been the one the negative energy had been focused on, and he needed to follow her lead. Right then, she was leading him away from a fight. He'd follow her anywhere, even if his instincts whispered it could be the wrong way.

"Let's forget him for now and get this job done for your boss," she said, sounding almost back to her normal self. Almost. "I'm in the mood for a little quiet time back at the cabin."

Translation—her wolf wanted to hole up in her den and hide from the world. And though Deus wanted to trust her words instead of his instincts, he couldn't. Something in her eyes told him this wasn't the first time she'd been told she wasn't welcome somewhere. And that thought made him want to dig through whatever records he could find to figure out where she came from. He'd promised her he wouldn't, but if people were after her, if some Alaskan pack wolf recognized her enough to demand she leave town, he needed to know why.

The fates help him, but he'd do anything to protect her, including breaking his promise to her.

Fourteen

The phone weighed on Deus' hand. He needed to call Luc, to tell him about what had happened in town, but he didn't want his mate to overhear the conversation. She'd seemed a bit more off-balance since they'd gotten back, a little less herself.

Running into that shifter could have been what set her off. The fear he instilled, the unease. Or the trigger for Beautiful's descent into herself could have been being trapped in a cabin usually reserved for poor pack wolves. She had no trust in pack, no faith in that sort of community. Her parents had pulled her away from hers—Deus had to assume there was a good reason for that. Reasons he didn't know how to combat.

Deus didn't know what to do to keep his mate safe and happy. How to chase away the ghosts that followed her. He needed advice on what would settle her wolf, which meant asking Luc. Even if doing so caused him to fuck up the mission he was in Alaska to complete. Which seemed to be an actual possibility.

Luc had texted twice since Deus had brought Beautiful back to the cabin in the woods. Deus should have answered his Alpha, but he'd been obsessed with getting the internet up and working so he could research, and once the satellite dish was installed and receiving data, he'd ended up focused on his mate. It was hard to resist her, harder to resist his need for her.

So he'd waited for the right opportunity. Her need to shower for a second time that day had been it, so Deus stepped outside while Beautiful headed for the bathroom. As soon as he reached the tree line—figuring a little extra space would keep the conversation private—he pulled up Luc's contact info and took a deep breath, pushing aside the unsettled sensation that had been haunting him. By the fates, did he feel as if he were drowning.

"Tell me," Luc said, not even giving Deus time for a greeting.

"Nothing yet. We spent the day in town but didn't find out anything about the pack. We had a run-in with someone I assume is from it, though."

"And?"

"He didn't like my mate. Said she wasn't welcome here."

"So she knew him?"

"No, that's the weird part. She said she's never been up here and never met the guy, but he definitely seemed to know something about her."

"Have you found out more about *her* yet?"

Like her name, where she was from, her family or pack info…all the things Deus shouldn't be looking up about her. "Not much."

"That's not nothing."

It wasn't. "My gut tells me she's an Omega."

A powerful female shifter considered a gift to any pack they were born into. Something shifters admired, honored, adored…and fought wars over. A variety of wolf thought to be a long-lost relative of the Dires. The female version.

Luc didn't argue the assumption. "Considering the rest of the brothers have found their mates in Omegas, that wouldn't surprise me. A gift to a pack from the fates, but without a pack behind her. There's a backstory there." Luc's voice had taken on that rough edge, the one that told Deus the shifter was getting pissed. Deus couldn't blame him. Something about Beautiful's story sat wrong with him. Worried him. Made him wonder how bad the truth could be.

He was almost afraid to find out. "I'm hoping she'll fill me in. Eventually."

"She doesn't trust packs, does she?"

Understatement. "No."

"Does she know about ours yet?"

"Negative."

"Tell her. Soon. A woman who's been abused by a pack in any way will have trust issues. Your not telling her will exacerbate them."

"I'll tell her." Deus would, too. Soon. He had to. "Now, how's your end of the mission going?"

Luc sighed, an unusual sound to hear from the shifter. "There's something wrong with the way they treat their packmates here, Asmodeus. Something in the way they dominate one another that makes my wolf uneasy. Keep a close eye on your mate."

Mate. The word sent his mind tilting slightly off axis. But the idea that the local pack could be a threat to her, even if the very idea of someone dominating a woman like Beautiful made him want to laugh, snapped him back to the task at hand. Luc had an almost preternatural sense when it came to the members of his pack—that included the women mated into it. He also knew when things were going wrong around him, and if he felt the need to mention a potential danger combining these shifters and Deus' mate, Deus knew better than to ignore him.

"What do you mean, there's something wrong with the way they treat their packmates? Is this focused on the women? Are they abusing them?"

"I can't get too close to the pack without them sensing me, so I'm trying to stay out of their way. That said, I haven't seen any women, so I don't know for sure what they are or are not doing."

"We didn't see any in town either."

"No?"

"No. I hadn't noticed, but Beautiful did."

"It's this pack. I can feel it, but I can't pin them down on anything. Whatever they're doing isn't new, though. There's an aged sort of veil over the instinct, one I'm having trouble seeing through. That's why I need you to find me intel on them."

"I'm looking. We went all through town but found nothing unusual."

"Except the shifter who knew your mate."

Fuck, that thought still pissed him off. "Yeah. Except him and his warning."

"Are you sending her home?"

Deus nearly grunted as pain lanced through his chest, and his wolf whined at the very thought. He should—intellectually, he knew putting her ass on a plane back to New York would probably be the right decision. But he didn't like the thought of being away from her. At all. Something inside of him—some instinct beyond just the mating itself—told him he needed her to stay close to him. He refused to disobey that feeling.

"No. She'll stay with me."

"Even if she doesn't want to?" Luc simply chuckled. "I never thought I'd see you mated, Asmodeus. I especially never thought I'd see you as demanding and controlling as Beelzebub."

Bez…the first Dire Wolf to find his mate in an Omega shifter named Sariel. Also, one of the most domineering souls he'd had ever met. To know Luc saw him in the same light almost made Deus cringe. Almost, but when it came to his mate, Deus didn't care if he seemed overbearing. Her safety was his only priority.

"Yeah, well…" Deus had no other words. No possible argument. And he didn't feel like searching for one.

"The mating haze is strong for you two."

Deus still didn't quite believe in the haze, but the lust he felt for his mate—the way he wanted to touch her all the time and keep her by his side—definitely seemed intense. "We have a strong connection."

"Sure. Call it that." Luc's throaty chuckle told him all he needed to know about his Alpha's thoughts.

"I'll keep digging for information on this place. Maybe hit up the library tonight and look through old newspapers and town records if they have them on microfiche or even paper versions."

"That's your personal version of hell."

No fucking lie. "Yeah, but I'll have my partner in crime with me, so it won't be all bad."

"You say that now. Once you're elbow-deep in old paper and your fingers are covered in ink, you'll change your story."

Never. "She'll make the moment worth it."

"So far gone. You and your—wait. What's happening?"

Deus held the phone, keeping his eyes on the little cabin, hurrying toward it as every one of his senses lit up. Something had just gone wrong. He felt it in his bones, could almost smell it on the air around him. And if bad news was about to come his way, he wanted to be close enough to his mate to protect her. So he ran.

Luc suddenly growled low, the sound jarring. "The pack is on the move. Stay put at your cabin for now and go to town again tomorrow. I'll call if anything seems to be heading your way."

"Are you in their way? Do you need backup?" Because no Dire fought alone unless he wanted to. That had always been a guiding light for the group

"I'm fine. I've been keeping my distance so as not to draw more chaos into their group. You stay at the cabin with your mate."

"Understood. Be safe."

"You too, brother."

Deus ended the call and headed inside, zeroing in on the sound of the water running in the small bathroom at the back. But before he turned that way, he darted to the couch where his laptop sat. A few keystrokes and he had the satellite internet connected and the web at his fingertips. It took him less than a minute to access the records he so meticulously kept, took him a little longer than that to image search his mate.

The first match wasn't her alone—it was a family picture. One taken in front of what looked to be a shack much like the cabin he sat in. Three people stood before the structure— he recognized his mate as the youngest. The child.

The fates help him for breaking his promises to her, but he had only wanted to keep her safe. The past he found wouldn't help him with that. It would only hurt her when she found out he'd betrayed her. He closed the connection and slammed down the lid of his laptop. He was the biggest asshole in the world. And someday, he'd have to admit what he'd done.

That he'd seen her humble childhood.

That he knew her name was Zoe.

Fifteen

The warm water of the second shower of her day pounded Zoe's stiff muscles, but it did nothing to settle her mind.

You're not welcome here.

She couldn't stop hearing those words repeating in her head. Why her? She hadn't been lying when she'd told Alaska she didn't know who that shifter was, but he'd certainly seemed to know her. An uncomfortable thought for sure. But also, why *here*? She'd never been to Alaska, never even heard of the Brooks Range or this region. She'd certainly never been involved with a pack from the area. The fact that in this place, in this town, there was someone who seemed to know her shook her to her core. For the first time since she'd stepped out of the car at the airport in New Jersey, she wondered if she should have come at all. Perhaps she should have left Alaska to his great north adventure and stayed in the city where she could blend in.

But then she would have missed so much time with her

new mate. Time she was actually enjoying. Time she wanted more of.

Alaska had skipped the shower with her, to Zoe's dismay. He'd grabbed her ass, run his knuckles across her pussy, and pouted like a schoolboy when she'd asked him to join her. He'd said he needed to call his boss and make sure the satellite he'd set up was working. Something about research he needed to do. The man and his computers…she couldn't compete. So she'd headed off to the bathroom alone, and she'd tried to catch her breath and resettle her wolf. Without success, unfortunately. No matter how much she attempted to push away the fear that strange shifter had instilled in her, she couldn't. The urge to run, to disappear back into the concrete jungle she called her home, was strong.

Zoe jumped when the shower curtain suddenly slid to one side. Alaska stood there, naked and hard, looking almost feral in his intensity. Those ice-green eyes appeared darker, his muscles larger, as he growled low in his throat.

"You okay?" he asked.

"Yeah. Just…distracted." Not the right word for how she felt, but it would work. It had to because she simply didn't have it in her to dig deeper for the truth.

Alaska stepped into the shower and closed the curtain before wrapping his arms around her from behind. Somehow, that move made things so much better. To be in his hold—her back against his chest, his lips nuzzling her neck—fulfilled everything she needed. Warmth and comfort, support and safety. Home.

He kissed his way down her neck to her shoulder and gripped her harder. Stronger. Pulling her tightly against him as he asked, "Want to tell me about that wolf?"

If he hadn't been supporting her with his body, she might have trembled at the thought of the man. "I already told you, I don't know who he is."

"You looked scared."

Zoe didn't feel fear often, but she was woman enough to admit when she did. "I *was* scared."

She turned to face Alaska, placing her hands on his chest. Keeping their bodies close as the water and steam warmed the space around them. "I'm still scared. A giant shifter in a tiny, man-filled town I've never been to singled me out as someone undesirable, and I have no idea how he knew anything about me. That's frightening."

Alaska growled, his arms like steel bands around her. "I would *never* let anything happen to you."

She wanted to believe him, wanted it more than anything. But people lied…shifters lied. And Alaska…well, she still didn't even know his real name, did she? The fates had brought them together, but that didn't mean he wouldn't try to deceive her. She'd been down those roads before, just without a mating bond between her and the other party. The journey had always ended in a mess of varying degrees.

"What are you thinking about?" Alaska asked, sliding a hand down her back to cup her ass and rock her against him. Trapping his cock and teasing both of them with the subtle movements while still staying focused on their conversation. Quite the task, really, because she was quickly losing track of words as her body craved more touching. He was just so distracting.

"Talk to me, Beautiful."

There it was. The name he called her. The one that had somehow become not enough. It lacked the connection she craved, the intimacy. It wasn't her. She looked up only to find him staring at her. His face open, trusting, and honest. Filled with something that looked the way her heart felt. Connected.

"I don't even know what to call you," she whispered, the words and fear of what that meant loosening its hold on something inside of her. Giving her the courage to open up, to offer something of herself, as a way for the two of them to grow closer.

But Alaska didn't answer at first. Instead, he watched her, unblinking. Unmoved, it seemed. And then he pulled her closer, blocking his eyes from her gaze. "I like it when you call me Alaska. It's like our own private thing, more special than if you called me the same thing everyone else does."

Immediately, whatever had been loosened tightened right back up enough to break her of the spell she'd somehow fallen under. He *couldn't* feel the same draw to her if he wouldn't even admit his name. She was ready to tell him hers—to tell him everything—but if he wasn't, then she didn't want to risk her heart. Perhaps the mating call pulled stronger on her, or she fell for him a little faster than he'd reciprocated. Maybe he didn't trust her enough to tell her something as simple as his first name, a thought that made her gut clench hard. One she had to take seriously.

Whatever was happening, whatever place he was in compared to her, she'd be sure not to bring up such a thing again. She wouldn't push for more info, for that sort of intimacy. She'd keep things more casual and allow him to set the pace. She'd also keep an exit strategy in mind, just in case. Because from where she was standing, that non-answer of his might as well have been a gentle nudge toward the door.

But until Zoe felt the need to walk out of it, she had a hot, sexy wolf shifter in her arms. One who made her laugh and curled her toes with his kisses. One she still wanted to share a little time with. One who still rocked her body better than anyone else she'd ever been with. So she plastered on a smile and pulled out of his arms before dropping to her knees.

"Then I'll always call you Alaska." She licked the tip of

his straining cock, humming softly as she tried hard to ignore the ache in her chest. To push past the disappointment burning a hole in her gut. She might not ever truly get all of him, but this, she could have. This, she could do. Physically, he was hers. For now.

So she sucked him deep, tonguing the underside of his cock while she stared up at him. While she watched his eyes burn and his jaw go tight. While she held on to his thighs as he rocked back and forth, as he fucked her mouth. And when he finally slid deep enough for her to have to hold her breath, for her to feel him at the back of her throat, she growled long and loud. Letting the rumble build in her chest and vibrate through her throat.

His hands flew to her hair, tugging, directing her as she opened wider so he could push farther, slide deeper. So she could swallow him down as he growled her nickname and began thrusting in earnest.

He came in her mouth with a groan that practically shook the walls. Zoe swallowed what he gave her, still growling low. Giving him every bit of her attention to pull him through his orgasm. Only releasing him when his grip on her turned soft and his breathing leveled out.

"Fuck. That was surprising and amazing, Beautiful. Let's dry off so I can return the favor."

"Don't we have work to do?"

"The only work I plan on doing tonight has to do with my face and cock working that pussy. Come on. I've got some giving to do."

Zoe kissed the tip of his cock one last time before rising to her feet and letting him steal a kiss from her swollen lips. And as he picked her up and carried her out of the bathroom, as she laughed and clung to his broad shoulders, she tried not to think how much she'd like to hear him call her Zoe just once.

Tried hard to breathe past the crushing steel bands that had somehow found their way around her chest.

— —

Zoe woke up from a deep sleep with one word reverberating through her mind.

Poverty.

It had a smell to it, a feeling of filth and fear that stunk up everything around her. Zoe remembered it well, and the fact that she'd woken up in the middle of the night with that same scent in her nose and that same itch to her skin threw her into what she could only describe as a moment of utter and total desolation.

Move. Run. Take.

She rolled out of bed, unable to catch her breath. Unable to stop the sick from rising in her throat, the bile from coming up. A sense of hunger gnawed at her gut and made her mouth water from the upset. From the pang. She hadn't been truly hungry in a number of years, hadn't been without food for decades, and yet she felt it. That ache. That feeling of never having enough. Of never being satisfied.

Stumbling, half crawling across the floor, she lurched into the kitchen and grabbed the first thing she could get her hands on. Bread. A loaf sat on the counter, and Zoe tore into it without the patience to actually open the bag properly as she fell to the floor and backed into the corner. She didn't need to bother with the twisty thing anyway—her claws made quick work of the plastic. And then she ate, trying to fill the gaping hole in her gut. Stuffing slices into her mouth and swallowing them down even though they never settled her stomach. Never filled the emptiness within her.

If they can feed you, they can starve you, her mother had said. A thousand times in all situations, Zoe's mother made sure to remind her only child that when you gave up your power, you gave up your independence. No one fed her now, no one had that sort of control over her. But the memories of being poor, of living in a cabin similar to the one she had just woken up in, of being prey to others who were supposed to work with you as a family unit, they stuck with her. Scarred her psyche.

They made her hunger for something she never knew how to acquire.

"Beautiful?"

Zoe gripped the bread tighter, snarling, at first unable to look at Alaska as she stuffed another piece in her mouth. "Go away."

"What are you—" He froze, watching her with knowing eyes. With a look on his face that didn't seem to be pity. That was totally not what she was expecting to see there. Still, she couldn't deal with the memories clawing at her mind. Couldn't handle the stress of being stuck in the type of house she'd hated so much. Of ending up right back where she'd started. Trapped. Weak. Empty.

No.

Never.

Not again.

Alaska didn't say another word, though. He simply moved to the bank of cabinets and opened one, pulling down a jar before grabbing a butter knife from the drawer.

He crouched before her and offered what was in his hands. "Here," he said. "Peanut butter has more protein in it. It will fill you up faster."

Zoe looked from him to the jar and back again, searching out the trick. The joke. Waiting for him to pull the food away and laugh at her. To try to starve her. He never did, though. He stayed calm and steady, offering her the food. Never faltering in his sincerity.

She grabbed the jar and knife with shaking hands, curling farther into the corner. "Thanks."

"Let me know if you need anything else." He stood, giving her space. Not stopping until he was halfway across the room once more. "How bad was it?"

Zoe knew what he meant—knew exactly what he saw. *How bad was it?* The hunger, the poverty, the living as prey for those with more power and wealth? "The worst."

He nodded once, a low growl rumbling from his chest. "Get your fill and come to bed when you're done. We'll be in town tomorrow and can pick up more food. Whatever you want. Whatever you need."

And then he crawled into bed and went silent. Zoe felt the need to follow him, but her hunger won out. So she made herself a sandwich, and she ate until she didn't feel the filth crawling all over her anymore. Until she had the strength to keep the emptiness at bay once more.

Sixteen

As the sun came up the next morning, Deus slipped outside the cabin once more with his phone in his hand. He hadn't slept well. Hell, if he was being honest, he hadn't closed his eyes at all since he'd woken up in the bed alone. He may not have sat with Beautiful on that kitchen floor—had known instinctually she wouldn't want anyone to witness that—but he'd stayed awake. He'd listened while she stuffed herself with peanut butter and bread as if she hadn't eaten in a week. And he'd suffered right alongside her.

Her desperation had been torturous but not unfamiliar.

He'd seen shifters do the exact same thing before—had been around when Luc had gone over the deep end of his memories and lost his sense of self. His Beautiful had been hungry once. Not in a minor way—her hunger hadn't been the kind that came from eating late or skipping a single meal. She'd been starved, routinely deprived of the nourishment she needed, and her wolf still bore the scars of those days.

Someone had *starved* her.

The thought gutted him. Deus could have killed whoever had done it with his bare hands, without even needing his wolf speed or strength to help him. He could have destroyed entire cities in retaliation for that senselessness. But he would have to know her past to figure out who was to blame, and they weren't there yet. That trust hadn't fully formed. So all he could do, all he could think of, was to call his Alpha for advice. Because Luc had been starved once, too. For years. Back before the Dire Wolves knew how to work together, before they knew how to be a pack. Before they knew how to fight.

Still, the number was not an easy one to dial.

Luc answered before the first ring had cut off, his voice already deep and worried. "What's wrong with your mate, Asmodeus?"

Luc's supernatural sense in regards to the Dire pack and their mates didn't surprise Deus one bit. "She had a moment last night. An…incident."

"What kind of incident?"

Deus looked to the sky, hating himself for even telling anyone this. Knowing he needed to. "She woke up and ended up in the kitchen eating bread."

"Yeah?" Luc said, lengthening the word, not understanding the severity of the moment. The desperation in her actions.

"She didn't open the bag. I found her curled in the corner with her claws in the loaf and her wolf eyes staring back at me as she stuffed slices into her mouth." Deus licked his lips and sighed. "I don't think she could have stopped."

Luc grunted. "She's been starved before."

"Yeah."

"You think it was intentional?"

That someone purposely took food away from her to punish her or her wolf. The thought brought out his claws even as he remembered the picture he'd seen the day before. The one of her in front of a shack. "I don't know. Could have just been neglect."

"Either way, her wolf is unsettled. I can sense that and your discomfort with it."

"Discomfort is an understatement."

"I can only imagine." Luc stayed silent for a moment, breathing softly. Deus gave him the time he needed, knowing the man was likely processing his own experiences and drawing from them. Finally, Luc asked, "Are you sure she should stay here?"

That was an easy question to answer. "Definitely. She needs someone to take care of her."

"Sounds as if she'd been taking care of herself just fine."

Deus couldn't argue that point. "She's staying with me, but how should I handle the eating thing? What do I do to make it better?"

"Feed her," Luc said, as if it was the simplest thing in the world. "Whatever, whenever…her wolf will settle eventually when she understands that you're going to make sure she has the basics she needs. Just keep her fed and safe."

Something so simple for a woman who was anything but. That he could do, though. He'd rob the only grocery store in town if he needed to keep her satiated.

"I'll do that."

"And go to town today. Take your mate on a research expedition and dig deeper."

Deus planned to answer his Alpha, but words failed him at that moment. The woman in question came walking out onto the porch, looking like an angel in the early morning glow. Beautiful's eyes met his, and everything around him disappeared. Damn, she was perfect. And his. All fucking his. His heart ached to be close to her, and his body seemed to come alive at the thought of touching, tasting, feeling, and loving up on his woman.

Why was he so far away?

"Deus. Focus."

Oh, right. The phone call.

"Whatever you say." Deus nodded at his mate, catching her eye as he moved toward her. Fighting the urge to hang up and run to her simply because she had looked his way.

"Be safe out there. Keep your eye on your female."

"I fully intend to."

Beautiful cocked her head, certainly hearing his side of the conversation, likely hearing Luc's as well. Didn't matter—let her know. Deus was growing weary of keeping things from her. He was also growing tired of not having her in his arms.

"Call me when you get back," Luc said before ending the call. Deus pocked his phone and closed the distance between him and his mate. The need positively roaring through his veins.

"What's wrong?" she asked when he reached the porch. He chuffed and reached for her, too afraid to open his mouth and growl at her. Too on edge to stay away. She didn't seem upset at his response, though. She grabbed his arms and frowned up at him as he grabbed her and pulled her into his hold for one long, tight hug.

He hated to let her go when it was done, though he loved getting a closeup look of her in her silky bathrobe that clung to every curve. "You look amazing this morning."

"That's not what has you upset."

"No, it's not. Did you hear the end of that conversation?"

"You're supposed to keep your eye on me."

"Right. Because my boss thinks the pack could be dangerous somehow."

"So are we stuck here again?"

Because Luc had told them to stay put the night before. "No. We don't need to stay here." Deus leaned closer, holding her gaze. "We'll likely spend the afternoon in town. Do you have everything you need for this morning?"

"I'll be fine." She darted a look toward her feet, likely knowing he meant food. That he remembered the night before. He didn't want her embarrassed or humiliated by what he'd seen, but he also wouldn't abide with her ever wanting for something as simple as food. He was, at his base, a wolf. He could bring down food in the forest if his mate needed it.

"You're sure? I'll take care of whatever you need me to, Beautiful. I promise you that."

"I'm okay. Really. Last night was…"

Deus hated the almost pained look on her face. "It was horrible, but we made it through. Right?"

She smiled softly. "Yeah. We did. Thank you."

"Don't thank me for caring. Now, we've got a few hours before anything is even open in town. What do you want to do?"

She looked past him, not seeming convinced by his words but not arguing either. "Can we go for a run? I'm feeling a little claustrophobic in there."

That sounded far better than counting down the minutes until they had to dig through the stacks at the local library. "A run would be perfect, but we can't go too far."

She shot him a cocky smirk. "Afraid someone will try to take me away from you?"

The very thought inflamed him. "No. I'm afraid I'll have to slaughter a pack for even trying."

Beautiful just shook her head, as if she didn't believe him. As if she truly thought he was exaggerating. He wasn't, and he really hoped he never had to prove that fact in front of her.

They stripped off their clothes and shifted, jogging through the woods at a casual sort of pace. Deus followed her lead, staying close on her heels but letting her decide where to go and how fast. Not wanting to crowd her.

Giving both of their wolves a chance to stretch their legs and their senses.

The forest felt calm to Deus—no indication that there was danger lurking in the deeper shadows, no sense of wrongness coming from the area. Still, he kept his attention focused on his mate and all that surrounded her. No way could he make a mistake now. He had to be battle ready, fully equipped and ruthless in his protection of her. He had to be prepared to take out any threat to her.

When they reached the top of the hill overlooking a vast, partially frozen lake below, Beautiful shifted human once more. Naked, sitting in the snow as if it wasn't cold and wet against her skin, she looked like some sort of sexy fairy nymph. One who frowned as she looked out over the forest below. One who seemed surrounded by a sadness he couldn't wish away. One he needed in his arms more than he needed to breathe, so he shifted as well and sat down behind her, pulling her into his lap.

"What are you thinking about so hard?" he asked once he had her exactly where he wanted her.

"This place. The pack here. All the things that could be going on with them that might make your boss tell us to stay put yesterday."

"He's protective."

"Why?"

Deus wasn't sure how to answer that. Why? Because he was. Always had been, always would be. Because they were pack, and pack took care of one another. Somehow, he didn't think that answer would suffice. "We've been friends for a long time."

"How long?"

Over a thousand years. "Lifetimes."

"That's awfully vague."

"Perhaps, but we're still getting to know one another.

We can be more specific another time." He leaned in to nuzzle her neck, breathing her in. Kissing from her ear to her shoulder and back. The pull to mate with her grew, the need to touch and taste and scent every inch of her hard to resist. Maybe the mating haze, though he was still not convinced, or perhaps simply his lust for her burning through him. Whatever it was, he had a sudden and intense need to know her inside and out, to learn everything about her, and to tell her everything about him. His name, the setup of his pack, the legends of the Dire Wolves…everything. And he wanted to start with something so simple, something she'd already brought up. Something basic. "Tell me your name, Beautiful. Give me that much, and I'll do the same."

Her body went stiff, and her voice sounded thicker as she replied, "I like it when you call me Beautiful. It's like our own secret thing, remember? Alaska and Beautiful…we don't need to know the rest."

They did, especially if he was going to find out more about her. If they were going to grow closer as a unit. He'd told her he liked using the nicknames because it was like a secret between them just the day before, but he hadn't meant to never share more with her. He'd intended to open up about his past so she could be honest about hers, just not at that exact time. Perhaps he'd messed up that moment—perhaps her saying she didn't know what to call him was more of a request for him to tell her something instead of a moment of needing reassurance. Something he'd missed. But he couldn't fix his mistake so he didn't argue, choosing to focus instead on simply holding her in his arms as the minutes passed. On taking whatever affection he could get…because he suddenly had a sinking feeling in his gut that this quiet intimacy wouldn't last for long.

Seventeen

*Z*oe could only assume that something had cracked between them after their run. Or perhaps something about their connection had shifted. Alaska barely spoke to her once they returned to the cabin, spending hours on his laptop instead. He stared and typed and stared some more, his satellite internet connected and obviously working as he searched for...she had no idea what. Whatever it was, he didn't seem too happy about the information he found.

So she spent her morning entertaining herself. First, with various games she could play on her phone, and later—once she'd retreated to the bed alone for the first time since they'd arrived—she tried to lose herself in a book. It didn't work.

Instead, she lay there watching him work. Noting every tic and quirk, every bit of body language she could make out. The way he hunched over the glowing screen and the speed with which his fingers moved over the keyboard. The stiff set of his shoulders and the firm line of his jaw. How his thighs bulged from the way he sat and his ass filled out the back of his jeans. And as she felt sleep tugging her away from her vigil, she understood the empty feeling inside of her chest.

She missed him.

Missed his cuddles and his laugh, his touch and his attention on her. Fear of losing such a fragile connection had wedged itself solidly between them, and she had no idea how to dislodge it.

"We should definitely head to town soon," he said suddenly as he closed his laptop and looked her way. "We can grab lunch, and then I'd like to get a start on the research we need to do."

She sat up, her mind groggy and her body slow. Had she fallen asleep? The emptiness that had started that morning yawned inside of her, making her believe she had. "You didn't find anything yet?"

He looked away, something close to regret flashing across his face. "Not what I needed, no."

The hair on the back of her neck stood up, and her instincts flared. *Do not trust* echoed through her head even as she rose to her feet and headed for the bathroom. The feeling of unease, the warning brewing in her blood, didn't end either. Not while she readied herself for the day, not even on the ride into town while they chatted about the weather and the beautiful views. She'd thought that something had cracked between them. She'd been wrong—it had been broken. She just wasn't sure what that something was yet— or if there was any possibility of repairing it.

She also had to deal with being back in a town where a stranger had told her she wasn't welcome. The anxiety of another run-in with the big shifter only fueled her inner turmoil. Everything about the day felt off, everything about the moment wrong. Had she been home and on a job, she'd have backed out. Would have canceled and tried another time. But she wasn't home, and she couldn't back out. All she could do was follow her mate and hope her instincts were wrong. That everything about the afternoon wouldn't turn out to be a mistake.

"My boss mentioned that the pack treats women oddly," Alaska said as they mounted the stairs at the library, heading for the records room in the attic. Obviously clueless to her inner torment. "We need to look for records of reasons why that might be—news reports, anything odd about town politics, stories that don't quite add up from the entire region."

"All this work because the local pack treats women the same way every other one seems to."

He jerked, nearly stopping. A telling physical reaction to what she'd said, though not one she knew how to interpret.

"Not all packs are the same, Beautiful."

His tone set her wolf on edge, though she restrained the beast enough to keep her voice from rumbling with the force of her growl. "No, but most still treat women like commodities. Something they've bought and whose value fluctuates over time depending upon what the men need from them."

Alaska grunted in response. No words, no true answer. Just that one rough noise. The conversation seemed to be over.

They spent the next several hours poring over old microfiche reels and even older copies of papers from a hundred-mile radius. Dust covered everything, dancing in the sunlight streaming through the windows and causing the world to fade a little. Zoe grew more anxious in the grime, and her mate definitely seemed to hate it as well. A fact that seemed to turn his mood more sour as the day ran on.

"Fuck, I need my computer," he muttered as he yanked a page up and flipped it over. He'd been reading through the old, yellowed newspapers from the county herald—

apparently, that wasn't going well. "I can't put my finger on it, but I've seen something like this before. The lack of info, the isolation, the women not having any face in local media. You still haven't seen a single picture of a woman in any of the files or records?"

"Not a one. Only men from the area." Zoe scanned through more microfiche, the machine whirring as the images and text flashed across the screen.

Alaska suddenly growled and slammed his fists onto the table. "I can't remember what pack this reminds me of."

"Memory fading in your old age?"

He huffed, the wrinkle of newsprint telling her he'd gone back to searching through the paper. "When you're over a millennium old, things start to go, I guess."

Once again, the hair on the back of her neck stood up, and something within her told her to run. Millennium, he said. That was a thousand years. Shifters didn't live that long, at least none that she'd ever heard of. He was either lying, exaggerating, or…immortal. None of which made for a comforting explanation. She knew better than to ask him about his comment, though. He didn't trust her enough to tell her his name—he certainly wouldn't trust her to explain how he'd lived so long. Or even *if* he'd lived so long.

Alaska didn't seem to notice her shock, though. He paid no attention to her at all, it seemed, as he continued muttering. To her, to himself, she couldn't tell.

"Over the years, we've dealt with just about every pack on the globe. Every continent, every country, even ones that no longer exist. We have records of it all. I just have to access them and compare traits. Maybe run an algorithm that will seek out keywords or something. That might work."

He tossed the newspaper aside and ran a dirty hand through his hair, looking completely lost and unfocused. Her mate disheveled and pained was something Zoe hadn't been prepared to witness, something her inner beast couldn't stand to see. He looked so beaten down, as if this task had gotten away from him and he didn't know how to get back on track. As if he felt failure looking overhead. His obvious distress clawed at her gut and made her want to fix everything for him.

If only life was that easy. "So…are we leaving, then?"

He looked up as if he'd forgotten she was there. As if she'd somehow surprised him. "What? Leaving?"

She didn't understand the worried look on his face or the sudden gleam in his eyes. Didn't understand it at all. She also didn't like it. "To go back to the cabin. You said you needed your computer."

"Right. Yes. Of course."

Distracted. No other word encompassed the way he acted or the look he wore. The man seemed completely focused elsewhere, and Zoe felt the need to stay completely focused on him. To take care of him as he struggled with remembering whatever it was he needed to. Which was probably why she never heard the other wolves coming up the stairs until they were already in the attic room.

"I told you that you're not welcome here," the guy from the day before said, looking mean and ready to fight as he zeroed in on her. Zoe's stomach dropped and her wolf perked up, inquisitive and wary. Not sure whether to run or stay put.

Alaska took the decision away from her by moving to block the men from looking her way. "She's with me, and we're just here for a few days."

"Your Alpha said the same thing, yet he's been sniffing around our pack for weeks."

Alpha. The word slammed into Zoe's gut like a wrecking ball into a decrepit, useless building. Alaska was a pack wolf— something he'd neglected to tell her. No, not neglected…lied to her about. Even after she'd made her feelings about packs clear, he'd kept that secret. Had continued to call the man who'd sent him to Alaska his *boss*, not his Alpha. There was no denying that deception.

Shame and anger crawled through her, making her want to strike out at the man before her. How dare he not tell her his truth? And she'd allowed it—had let him hedge his comments about packs and leaders as she'd ranted. Had accepted him saying boss even when she knew there was a deeper meaning behind the word. Had looked away when he'd refused to even share his name with her.

She'd done this to herself, and she'd be the one to fix it.

"You have an Alpha?" she asked, raising an eyebrow when Alaska turned to glare her way.

"Not now, Zoe," he whispered, his voice pitched low. Barely loud enough for her to hear him, let alone for any other wolves in the room to make out his words. But she did hear him. She heard him loud and clear.

Heard the name he shouldn't have known

Her heart stopped before kicking into high gear. Gut check number two—dishonesty. All these days, all this time as Beautiful and Alaska had been a lie. He *knew* her but hadn't told her anything about himself. He'd never shared information equally. He'd gone against her wishes, looked up information about her, and manipulated her.

She'd never felt so stupid or foolish in her life. Alaska wasn't Alaska, but he was a pack wolf. And a liar. Two things she couldn't stand. Two things she refused to be mated to.

Zoe pasted a smile on her face and raised her hands, making sure the two men guarding the stairs could see her. "You know, I can end this easily enough. Let me get past you since you're blocking the stairs, and I'll head for the airport."

The shifter from the day before nodded once, the two men moving to the side as if to give her a path out of the attic. One she planned to take advantage of. She pushed past

Alaska, trying hard not to look at him. Not to touch him. Not to feel the rage his actions had incited in her. But the man wasn't going to let her go so easy.

Alaska reached for her arm, pulling her to a stop. Zoe spun and let her wolf free, snapping at his touch and yanking her arm away from him with a growl. He stared, wide-eyed.

"Beaut—" He froze. She could only assume he'd realized his mistake. That she'd put together the fact that he knew her real name and had used it. Or he was just as good of an actor as he was a liar. Something she wasn't in the mood to figure out.

She stood to her full height, raised her chin, and gave him the sauciest wink and grin she could manage. "It's been fun, but I'm going back to the city. You can finish up with your *Alpha* on your own."

She spun and walked away, giving the two shifters a wide berth when she reached the stairs. She hated turning her back on the men, but she had no choice. She needed to get the hell away from them all, and that meant leaving them behind. Not that they let her. Or, at least, Alaska didn't. He followed right behind her, staying two steps back as she hit the bottom floor and headed for the street.

"Zoe, wait. I didn't mean to—"

"To what?" she asked, spinning and growling at the man who wouldn't let her leave. "Break my trust? Lie to me? Ignore my wishes and try to control the situation?"

He sighed, looking completely out of sorts. "Yeah. All of that."

"Well, you did. And then you refused to give me even a tiny piece of the same knowledge about yourself. I won't deal with deceit, not from any man."

"Just wait," he said as he reached for her again. As he tried once more to restrain her, to stop her from doing what she wanted to. As he attempted to force her hand.

Just like a pack wolf to be so controlling.

"I don't need to wait." Zoe stepped back, putting more space between them. More space she couldn't believe she even wanted after the few days of needing to be close to him. Of trusting him with her body...and her heart, sadly. She was such an idiot.

Not anymore though. "I don't need to know your name to know enough about you. I don't want a pack wolf, and I certainly don't want a liar. Mating pull or not, this isn't going to work for me, so I'm leaving."

Alaska roared, but she simply turned and walked away. Ignoring him and his anguish. It could have been an act, for all she knew. Could have been part of his show. His trickery.

No matter how much it hurt to leave him, how bad her wolf whined and clawed at her mind to give him another chance, she couldn't. She couldn't risk her freedom on a man who didn't even have the moral compass to be honest with her. Didn't have the guts to tell her his real name. The fates had been wrong about them being kindred souls—it'd happened before. She'd seen bad matches leading to lifetimes of sadness and abuse when she'd still been with her last pack. No way would she follow that path. Her heart may have wanted him, her body too, but her head ruled on this one. Her heart would get over it.

Or so she hoped.

Eighteen

Deus paced across the small cabin, his wolf whining and growling on every turn. She'd left. His beautiful mate, his Zoe, had actually left him. She hadn't even let him drive her back to the cabin, choosing to walk out of the library and walk to the airport instead. His instincts screamed to follow her—to track her down and argue his case until he convinced her to come back with him. Or to simply cart her back to the woods to stay with him. His wolf practically demanded it, but he couldn't. Wouldn't. Sure, he could go after her. He could follow her to the airport, take away her agency to make her own decisions, and drag her hot little ass back to his bed. He could—but she'd hate him forever if he did.

He couldn't live with that thought.

His phone pinged, and he practically snarled at the device. Luc again. The man had been texting him every few minutes since Deus had watched Zoe walk away from him. His Alpha probably sensed his distress, the freaky psychic fucker tended to know when one of his packmates was off-kilter. And losing his mate had definitely made Deus feel off-kilter. But he had no time for all the "what's wrong?" and "why are you distressed?" and "what the fuck is happening?" messages. He needed to think, to sort through his feelings and find the connection to Zoe so he could focus on that. He needed to figure out how to win her back, even if that meant letting down his Alpha—and by default, his pack—and chasing after her.

If only he'd told her about himself. If he'd explained about being a Dire Wolf and what that meant in terms of family and pack. He'd been so distracted by her—both physically and in researching everything he could about her—that he'd completely misstepped in their relationship. He should have focused on earning her trust. She wouldn't have been so surprised then, wouldn't have been shocked or felt betrayed by him when those bastards had brought up his Alpha. Fuck, if he'd just told her his goddamned *name,* this likely wouldn't be happening.

Another ping. Another text from Luc. This one about the local pack. *They're on the move again.*

"Not fucking now," Deus said with a growl, tossing his phone across the room to land on the bed. Why the man had such a hard-on for that pack, Deus still didn't understand. He also didn't have enough energy to worry about it. He had to stay focused on Zoe, had to try to reach the bond between them that they hadn't yet solidified. Was she gone already? Had his plane taken off with her inside of it, whisking her back to New York? Had he lost her?

No. He refused to think that way. His mate wouldn't walk away—not for good. True, she was the daughter of a con man, something he'd learned in researching her history, but she'd been real with him the past few days. True and honest and present. Zoe was a strong, independent wolf who took no shit, and he'd lost her because he hadn't respected that fact enough. Hadn't trusted her or allowed her to trust him. Hadn't given her a reason to. She'd been his for a handful of glorious days, and he'd lost her because he was an idiot.

No more.

Deus grabbed his laptop and settled on the couch to research more. He needed data to figure Zoe out, so he opened the websites he'd found previously and started reading again. Last time, he'd learned the barest of details—a name, age, and former pack information. This time, he dug deeper. Into her past, her family, her history. He should have felt guilty for looking when he'd promised not to, should have chided himself for betraying her trust *again*, but he had no other choice. He'd already fucked up—he needed to figure out a way to fix his mistake, which meant he needed to know more about her.

Ten minutes and fifteen text messages received—all most likely from Luc—later, Deus finally found a picture in what had only been text so far. It was old and grainy, probably taken by his Dire brother Levi, who was the pack photographer and documented their histories visually more than any other pack member.

Similar to the first picture he'd discovered but better quality and closer. In it, Zoe stood beside her parents in ragged, tattered clothing with her hair hanging down and her hand by her mouth. Scared. Her mother held her other hand, chin up, looking so much like Zoe it hurt.

So much like Zoe.

A century later, and they could have been twins.

Deus looked again, blowing up the picture. Zoe was the spitting image her mother, and shifters didn't age like humans. Had her mom been alive, it would have been near impossible to tell them apart. Would have been like looking in the mirror for the two women. Something clicked into place in his head, a feeling of dread and intuition settling over him as he tried to put the pieces together.

"You're not welcome here."

Not Zoe. Her mom. Maybe. Possibly. There was only one way to find out. Deus dug deeper, this time seeking information on the picture, on the dad, on the mom. Histories and pack records, details and legends about the family, plowing through random bits of information until he finally hit on one line. One remark about Zoe's mom that sent ice shooting down his spine.

Possibly born into Brooks Range, Alaska pack.

"Holy shit." He scanned the picture again, the pieces finally sliding into place. The anger from the local wolf directed at Zoe, the weird sense that they knew her even though she didn't return the feeling. Her mom had come from the local pack, Zoe looked just like her mom, so the pack assumed Zoe was her.

Another ping sounded from his phone, and Deus grabbed it almost absentmindedly. Growling, trying to work out what could have possibly set a pack to banish a female of their own, he swiped the screen to life. Most messages were just as he'd expected—comments about the pack from Luc, messages of concern. The last one, though…one word. One simple request from Zoe that caused his wolf to explode from his skin with a snarl unlike any he'd ever issued.

One syllable that set his world spinning.

Help.

Nineteen

He lied to me.

That was all Zoe could think about as she hurried toward the airport. Alaska—not Alaska, not his real name, not that she knew his name because he wouldn't tell her even though he knew hers—had lied straight to her face. Her heart had cracked wide open when that truth dropped on her head, and she wasn't sure if she'd ever be able to put it back together again.

But her resounding pain at his betrayal wasn't her only concern, or at least, it wasn't her immediate one. She could survive a broken heart—she wasn't so sure she could survive the attack of a rabid wolf unless she got the hell out of this town. The local pack wasn't kidding around with their *you're not welcome here* line, and Zoe didn't want to push them too far. Especially without Alaska by her side to—

Nope.

Not going there.

Her mate had let her down. Had completely destroyed

her trust in him. Had manipulated her into thinking they were on even ground while really pulling strings to run the show. There would be no working, scheming, *or* fighting together. Ever.

Her wolf let out a plaintive howl at that thought.

"Quit whining," Zoe murmured to herself. Or to her inner wolf, really. The beast seemed far more upset about losing her mate than the possibility of an entire pack attacking them. Zoe would have assumed that the instinct to survive—the natural fight for life itself—would have overpowered everything else to the wolf. She would have been wrong. Mate beat all in the animal's world. Wonderful.

As she crossed the street and headed for the road that would take her to the airport, her neck tingled, the telltale sense of someone watching her strong. This town was too small, too quiet, and too lacking other women for her not to be noticed, which was the last thing she needed at the moment. She wanted to hide—to hole up in a den and let her wolf howl her sorrows to the moon, but she couldn't. Not yet, at least. Once she was home, back in the city where she could disappear, she'd give in to her need to wallow in the sadness that was her shattered heart. For now, she had to pretend she wasn't falling apart inside. Pretend she wasn't about to leave the man she'd not just been mated to but fallen in love with behind.

Yeah. Love. Of all the fucking luck.

Just the thought of flying away from Alaska—the man, not the state—made her feel worse. It killed her to think of leaving her mate, but there was nothing she could do. She refused to be with a liar. Refused to even contemplate the option. How could she? She knew what it was like to live with people who never told the truth. Who used and twisted and bastardized the concept of partnership and connection to get their way. She'd been taken from her family, caged, and starved, all so her *pack* could gain access to the powers she'd never understood. The ones she'd never learned to use. If her parents hadn't snatched her back and run, she'd likely have ended up in that cage for her entire life. She would have been nothing but a tool for someone else to use.

She didn't want that for her future.

She wanted trust and companionship, passion and security. Wanted to be a partner with someone, to work together and know they respected one another. Wanted to be independent while sharing her life with another.

Sadly, she wouldn't find that with Alaska.

Her wolf whined in her head, sending her thoughts and pictures of being with Alaska, talking with him. Of their time together so far and how they could still go back and try to get answers to why he'd betrayed them. Perhaps that would be the wolf thing to do—confront him about his deception and see what he had to say. Ask him about his life, his plans, and his pack. But Zoe couldn't trust his answers, so what was the point of being the mature one and initiating such a difficult conversation? The wicked, spiteful side of her—the part she usually kept hidden deep down—said fuck that. Their love story was over, *finito*, happily ever after canceled. No way back and no way forward either. Done.

And by the fates, did that thought hurt.

But pain ended eventually. Zoe needed to go home. Needed to get some breathing room. She didn't need to turn around and go looking for more heartache. Why give the man the chance to hurt her again? Hell, she never should have opened herself up to him in the first place. She'd fallen for that mate pull and let it tug her toward someone who would only drag her ass back to the life she'd already left behind. Back to the cage. Never again.

Zoe finally reached the airport—a much longer trek on foot than in a car, it seemed—and headed for the hangar. She could only hope Alaska hadn't done something shady like tell the pilot not to allow her to leave. She didn't even know if commercial planes flew out this way—she'd arrived on a private plane. Alaska's private plane.

"He'd better not try to stop me," she muttered as she reached for the door handle and yanked it open. She took one step inside, ready to yell for someone to help her, when she froze.

Wolves.

The smell of them permeated the air. So strong, so thick—as if a pack had bedded down in that very hangar for days on end. They had to be there somewhere in the shadows, watching her. Waiting. She couldn't run from them, couldn't hide either, because she'd been too caught up in her own thoughts and rage to think before she came barging inside. All she could do at that moment was keep moving forward, fake some confidence, and hope she made it out unscathed.

And maybe she could call for backup.

One text message—one word—was all she managed before the pack broke free from the dim corners of the open space and moved toward her as a unit. She tucked her phone away and watched them come, her only escape a plane at the other end of the building or the door she'd walked in, which she'd left slightly ajar by accident. Might be one heck of a happy accident if this went the way she had a feeling it would.

Dirty, scraggly, and hungry-looking, the pack stalked closer. Herding her back. Hunting her. Most couldn't hold eye contact, too weak of spirit to go up against her at that basic wolf challenge. A few growled, but all of them—every last one—seemed to be breathing way too hard for their level of exertion. Beyond the fact that they needed a shower, a change in attitude, and a little backbone, something wasn't right with them. And they were looking at her as if she were some sort of prize.

Shit, shit, shit.

As much as she hated to admit it, she was going to need some help. A lot of it. And she'd already sent for him. Alaska had better be on his toes if she had any hope of getting out of there alive, let alone unscathed.

The huge wolf she'd seen around town approached first, leading a band of six males. "I told you to leave."

Time to play up her attitude. She cocked a hip and raised an eyebrow while motioning to the room around her. "And I'm at the airport. Trust me, it's not because I like watching planes land."

The man growled low and deep, his eyes hard, his teeth showing as he said, "You're already late getting out of my town."

"I didn't realize I had a time limit." She rolled her eyes and moved as if to go around them, feigning a surety she definitely didn't feel. But the pack kept her half surrounded. Kept her away from the single plane at the far end of the building. Escape route number one, blocked. Route number two…definitely still an option, but she really wanted to fly the hell out of that town, not run back through it. "I'm trying to leave on that perfectly good airplane over there. Why don't you call off your dogs so I can?"

The way his lips turned up in a sneering sort of smile made her blood run cold and set every instinct she had for self-preservation on fire. "I think we'll keep you instead. Teach you a lesson, Dina."

It took Zoe a full two seconds to register the name he'd used. Dina…her mother's name. The woman who'd busted into the place where her daughter was being held captive and killed three wolves to get her out. The woman who'd figured out how to make something from nothing—from less than nothing—and pushed Zoe to do the same. The woman who'd told her from the time she was a tiny, scraggly child hanging off her hip to stay independent. *"Never trust a pack, baby. Their best interests will never line up with yours."*

Zoe hadn't even known what best interests had meant then, but she'd listened. Had absorbed the words, the fear, and the warning. If this pack knew her mother—a woman who'd never once mentioned spending time in Alaska— Zoe was in a lot more danger than she'd originally thought. Which was saying something, because she'd figured she was in some pretty ugly danger from the moment she'd walked into the hangar.

Tall, Dirty, and Psychotic took another step closer, and her world shattered before coming back together. Her wolf exploded from within her, sensing the danger and taking over without giving Zoe the chance to argue the move. She shifted without thinking about doing it, her claws scrabbling on the cement before she was even fully through the change. She wasn't the biggest wolf, not the best fighter either, but she was smart and fast. Something that had benefited Zoe in her job as a thief and would hopefully work to her advantage with the pack. At least, she hoped so. It needed to be enough to get her away from them because there was no way she could win in a true fight.

Only three wolves followed her as she slipped out the open door, which meant the rest of the pack was confident they'd be able to bring her back. That thought only added more fuel to her fear. No fucking way were they taking her alive. She'd run until her paws bled, fight until she had nothing left. Something about those wolves in there was wrong—sick. Something screamed at her to get the hell away from them as fast as she could. To never stop running.

To do whatever it took to stay out of their cage.

Zoe made it halfway across the tarmac when the sweetest sight she'd ever seen played out before her, the only thing that could have possibly brought her comfort in that moment. A deep silver wolf was running full out across the pavement, racing toward her with his teeth bared and his ears pinned back. Ready to dive headfirst into a fight. But this wolf wasn't dirty or scraggly—he was huge. Massive, really, with dark spots along his back, and hips and paws big enough to shake the earth. She knew that wolf—loved him, too. She didn't need to know his real name to know that Alaska had come to help her fight.

That huge wolf was truly the best thing she'd seen all day.

Zoe yipped once to get his attention and headed directly for him. He didn't stop when she reached him, didn't pause a beat. He barreled past her instead, snarling his warning to the men behind her. His growl shook her to her very core, and his paw strikes sounded like thunder as he ran straight at the three wolves chasing her. He was pissed, and she'd never been more grateful than in that moment to have such a strong and healthy mate.

For the first time, she was so very thankful for the mating bond pulling them together—not just any male had been paired with her, but a giant guardian of a male. A true warrior. He'd defend her because he saw her as *his*. As property he owned. And at that moment? Between being his and having to fight off an entire pack? She'd take the first option. Besides, she'd let him think whatever he wanted, let him believe he had some sort of control over her, so long as he got them out of there alive. The details could be worked out later.

Alaska slammed into the wolf closest to her without even pausing, sending the poor beast flying and immediately diving for the second. Her mate's teeth actually crunched as he bit into his adversary's neck. Zoe crouched in place, bouncing on the toes of her paws and watching the battle as Alaska tore his way through the shadows of what he truly was. His wolf skated and twisted, agile and strong in his movements. Aggressive and powerful. Winning from the start, while the pack wolves practically stumbled over themselves.

All except one.

The third wolf circled Alaska, looking as if he would mount a sneak attack on her mate. Something she couldn't abide. Alaska had come for her, had rushed into a fight to help her; she could at least return the favor. Instead of running off as her instincts told her to do, she dove at the wolf, knocking him off course and giving Alaska a heads-up that his flank wasn't protected. Her mate had the two on the ground—both likely dead from the look of things—when he finally spun and focused on the last one.

The third wolf shifted human, showing himself as the same man from town and the library. As weak, too, because he sprawled on the concrete, gasping for air. Obviously not in the shape necessary to both keep up with Zoe and fight off her mate. Thank the fates for small favors.

Alaska kept himself between the man and Zoe, rubbing his body against hers and making soft, breathy sounds in his throat. Chuffing. His wolf checking in on hers to make sure she was unharmed even as he kept up his guard pose. Zoe whimpered and nuzzled him right back, needing a moment to reconnect. Unsure what the next step would be and how the hell she was going to get out of town since the airport was overrun with the pack. And how she was going to leave Alaska behind again after feeling so relieved to see him in the first place.

She was distracted by her mate, which shouldn't have surprised her. But it did. Mostly because that lack of focus wasn't like her. She should have been watching the other wolf. Should have been paying attention.

She didn't, which was why his voice carrying across the cold Alaska air surprised her almost as much as his words did.

"Well, what do you know? Looks like the thief's got herself a Dire Wolf."

ooks like the thief's got herself a Dire Wolf."

The words pulled Deus up short. Fuck, this wouldn't be good. The second those words escaped the shifter's lips—a man the local pack called Rudkin, if his research was correct—Deus knew he was screwed. Again. Not even the scent of her so close, her wolf body brushing his, could calm the alarms inside his head.

He hadn't told Zoe about his lineage, hadn't gotten to explain how he and his Dire brothers had survived, how they had formed their pack. How they were who they were. She didn't yet understand all that went into his life because he'd failed to tell her any of it. There was no way Zoe would forgive him for keeping another secret from her.

Deus shifted human, keeping wolf Zoe close by his side. Ready to fight with fists if teeth and claw wasn't Rudkin's style. Ready to do anything to protect his mate, whether she wanted to be his or not.

"The thief's got herself more than just a Dire Wolf,"

Deus said, keeping his voice calm but strong. Not releasing Rudkin from his hard stare as he went for the only thing pack wolves like him understood—dominance. "She's got herself a mate, so don't fuck with her."

Rudkin grinned, looking both amused and treacherous all at once. Or possibly just unhinged. "She was leaving without you. Couldn't be much of a mating bond if you'd let her go all alone."

There was no *letting* her go—she wanted to leave. If he'd tried to stop her, he would have been ignoring her wishes. Would have been trying to control her. And though he'd do anything to keep her by his side, he knew Zoe would have hated him for it. She wasn't the type of woman to be okay with asking for permission. And Deus wasn't about to try to make her one.

Zoe weaved through Deus' legs, growling continuously. She didn't move even an inch away from him, didn't break the physical connection of her wolf body touching his human one. He tried to keep her behind him while she refused to hold still. Typical. At least she wasn't running anymore, though. That was something working in his favor. At least, he hoped it was.

Still, Deus wasn't done fighting for her freedom just yet. "You told her to leave, and she's leaving. You're getting what you want."

"It's too late," Rudkin screamed, his eyes blazing with a frenzied sort of energy that made Deus want to toss Zoe's ass on the plane and fly her out of there himself. "Already, the other Dire Wolf stalks our camp, gathering information to bring the Lycan Brotherhood here. Our pack, our lifestyle, will be over. And it's her fault. That bitch—" he pointed right at Zoe, who froze in her tracks "—is a curse on our pack. She always has been."

In for a penny, in for a pound. If digging his own grave

with his mate meant he kept her alive, he'd do it. He had to. Time to admit even more of his mistakes. "This isn't Dina. And even if it was, she never did anything to your pack besides leave it. Dina wasn't cursed—she was smart enough to run the fuck away from a pack like yours where anyone not seen as a higher dominant is subjected to abuse."

"We don't abuse the females."

"I find that hard to believe. Two hundred years of your pack making this region their home, yet there's no picture or mention of a female in the records. Not one…besides Zoe's mom, Dina."

Rudkin smirked. "We have almost forty males and two females in our pack. We keep the women away from others so they don't try to steal them away."

"You can't steal someone who doesn't want to leave in the first place."

The zeal returned to Rudkin's eyes, the fire of his insanity burning hotly. "They're our females, and they'll stay ours. We get to keep them both."

And suddenly, everything made sense. Luc's premonition of something wrong in the region, the fact that the pack had a strange and unsettling dominance dynamic, the overabundance of men in town. The pack had the only two women in the region, and they would stop at nothing to keep them.

And if his instincts were right, they also wanted his mate to add to their very limited collection.

Deus' stomach turned, his worry for the safety of those women growing with every second. His rage at the idea of some twisted fuckers taking away his mate to be some sort of pack slave burning bright.

"You can't have her," Deus said, letting his wolf growl over the words to make his point. "Whether she stays with me or not, Zoe is not yours to keep. She doesn't want to be here, doesn't want anything to do with your pack, so she's going home."

"If a female steps foot in our region, we get to keep her. That's the law."

"Your law is perverse."

"We had to do it. She cursed us." Rudkin pointed right at Zoe, an act that made Deus' wolf snarl and whip his body between the two. The beast could be the brawn—Deus needed to be the brain.

"Your pack has two females but no matings, right? Tell me something, brainiac. When was the last time the fates gifted someone in your pack with a true mate? It was likely Dina and her mate, Zesthial. Zoe's mom and dad, wasn't it?" Deus stepped forward, keeping his eyes locked on the other man's. Letting his wolf shine through to make sure Rudkin knew he was dealing with a much stronger animal. "You're the ones who are cursed, and it's not Dina's fault or influence. You betrayed the fates by your actions, and you continue to pay the consequences because you don't change."

"The fates gave you the daughter of a thief who leaves you behind at the drop of a hat. What did you do to deserve that?"

Deus shook his head, not falling for the deflection. Also not willing to let any blame land on his mate's shoulders for his situation. "I'll never deserve Zoe. I'll never be so arrogant as to see her as anything other than a gift bestowed upon me by the highest powers. One I need to cherish and respect, not control. See, that's why I let her leave without me. Because she wanted to. Because I have no dominion over her. I don't own her—I'm just thankful every time she grants me the gift of her presence."

Zoe shifted to her human self behind him, pressing her warm, soft body against his. Hanging on to his hips as she rested her chin on his shoulder. It felt so good to touch her again. The contact soothed something inside of him, even as his beast continued to stand in protection mode. Hard to the outside world, soft to his mate. That was the balance he needed to find. Aggression versus affection. He'd fight for that. He'd fight for her.

Deus let his hand fall to Zoe's thigh, squeezing the flesh. Gripping tight as he said, "She's mine not because I own her, but because she owns me. Everything I do is for her—her comfort, her safety, and her pleasure. *That's* how you treat a female, fated mate or not."

Rudkin looked as if he was about to say something, but a loud howl sounded from the woods nearby. He snapped his head in that direction, listening, his entire body on alert. Then he shifted. That same dark, scraggly wolf stood where Rudkin had lain, eyes bright but coat dull. Skinny, too. Far too skinny. He gave Zoe a final glare and growl, even as Deus snarled back at him, then turned and rushed off toward the hangar. Deus let him go, too worried about his mate to leave her side. Knowing he and Luc would take care of the problem with this pack eventually.

One yip from Rudkin was all it took to open the floodgates. Or the doors, as it were. The wolves of the Brooks Range pack streamed out of the hangar, all of them running for the woods, heading farther away from town. Those still alive, at least. The two Deus had killed lay on the ground, abandoned by their brethren.

But even two dead shifter bodies needing to be dealt with couldn't take priority away from his mate. Away from his need to protect her at all costs. Deus couldn't turn around, couldn't take his eyes off where the shifters had disappeared in case the pack came back. He still expected a fight, a war. Something coming for Zoe or him. And his mate—his strong, independent, beautiful mate—trembled against him. He could sense her fear but he could also feel it, and that only made his wolf that much more worked up. His rage at those bastards having scared her ratcheting the fury of both sides of his personality all the way up.

If the pack came for her, he'd be ready. He'd be a fucking force of nature against them. He'd get her out of this place and to safety, which was what his priority needed to be. Starting now.

"Are you okay?" he asked, giving her thigh another solid squeeze.

"I am now that you're here." Zoe sighed before slipping in front of Deus, rubbing her body against his as she did. Not breaking contact for a second. The wolf inside Deus appreciated that. The man appreciated how good she looked standing naked in the sun.

Do not fall into the lust of the mating haze.

As Deus fought to keep from dropping to his knees and worshiping her sweet pussy, Zoe stayed calm and focused. Looking up at him with gorgeous, dark eyes as she asked, "Did you mean what you said?"

That he saw her as a gift.

That he recognized no dominion over her.

That he respected her enough to let her go.

That she owned him.

"Every fucking word." Deus leaned down, pressing a soft kiss against her lips. One that quickly deepened as she pressed her hot little body to his and opened her mouth. He couldn't resist her, even as out in the open and unprotected as they were, so he grabbed her ass and tugged her in tight as he plundered her mouth. As he took advantage of all that she offered him.

When they finally broke apart, she took a deep breath and whispered, "My name is Zophiel, and I'm an Omega wolf born of the Northern Appalachian pack. That Alpha wanted my power, so he ordered the pack to take me away from my family, stuff me in a cage, and starve me as they tried to get my wolf to be the Omega. My mom busted me out and we ran. She never explained where she was from or their history before she and my dad arrived in the Appalachians, but I always felt as if she knew what that was like. To be taken—to lose control over your own life. She refused to let a pack lord over her, so we lived as nomads after the escape. My parents were killed by hunters when I was still an adolescent, and I've been alone for a lot of years. I'm afraid of having a mate and being in a pack."

Stunned. There was no other way to explain his reaction to her admission. To hearing her angel name given to him so freely. No, he was wrong. So very wrong. There was one more word. One more description of how she'd just made him feel.

Grateful.

Deus dragged her back against him, needing to feel more of her. To never let her go. She pressed her body against his, running her hands over his chest. Breathing with him as she settled into his arms. Where she belonged. But he couldn't let her take the leap of faith she just had and not respond, so he took a deep breath, and he told his own truth.

"I'm Asmodeus—my brothers call me Deus—and I'm a Dire Wolf. We formed a pack of sorts to take care of one another. My pack isn't like a normal one—we don't even all live in the same states—but when one of us is in trouble, the others come to help. No Dire fights alone unless he wants to, which is why we ended up in Alaska. My Alpha wanted help. I'm sorry I looked into your past and didn't tell you—I was worried, but that's not a good enough reason. I should have talked to you. I should have given you more of a chance to open up to me. I wasn't trying to control you, Beautiful… I was trying to keep you safe. I went about it all wrong, and I'll probably fuck up again another million times, but that's only because I care so fucking much. My pack—my family of

Dire Wolves and their mates—they will all care about you as family. You'll see—there is absolutely nothing those six men and the five other females in the Dire pack wouldn't do for you. And there's nothing I wouldn't do for you, Zophiel."

She nodded, her brow furrowed and her eyes thoughtful. "You forgot something."

His stomach dropped. "What's that?"

"You're my mate."

Fuck yeah, he was. Deus picked her up, carrying her toward the hangar. "Only if you'll have me."

Those deep, hazel eyes met his—so open and honest, they nearly stole his breath. But it was her words that caused his lungs to stop working.

"I don't know if I can do this."

"You can." He crouched a bit, needing to be in her face for this conversation. "*We* can. I'm not a pack wolf—I don't want you under my thumb and doing everything I say. I love that you're independent and strong. I love that your wolf plays dominance games with mine. All I want—we want—is the chance to be a part of your life."

"I might panic."

"We'll bring you peanut butter and calm you down."

"I prefer Spam."

Deus blinked. "Really?"

"Yeah."

"Then I'll buy it by the case."

She frowned. "I might try to run."

"We'll follow you. Not too closely though—just so we know you're okay."

"I like my job."

"I love your job. Especially if it means I get to see you in those skintight leather pants again. You can steal from me anytime so long as you're wearing those."

Zoe rolled her eyes and lifted her lips in a reluctant sort of smile. "I'm serious."

"So am I. About you and us and possibilities. And about not forcing you into anything. When you're ready—if you're ever ready—we'll talk about mating bites and claiming. Right now, I just want you with me. All the time."

She stared up at him for a long moment, her eyes locked on his. He could practically feel her worry, her indecision, her past experiences battling with her instincts. He had no idea what side of her was stronger.

At least not until she let out a breath and whispered, "Okay."

One word, and all was right in his world again. Two syllables, and his future was right there at his fingertips once more. He couldn't hold back another second. His lips met hers in a kiss that seared him down to his soul, that caused her to moan and wrap that hot little body around his in a way that should have been illegal. He wanted her. Wanted to fuck her right there in the hangar, wanted to lay her down on the concrete floor and plunge his cock so deep inside her as he gave her his claiming bite. As they finally completed their bond and became one. But he wanted her safe more, and that meant he needed to get her biteable ass on a plane and the fuck out of Alaska. Away from the pack that threatened her.

Away from him.

His wolf whined at the very thought. His human side knew it was the only way. "I'll send you your stuff."

"What stuff?"

"Your clothes. The things you brought with you. I'll send it on to you." Hopefully to Bez's place in Texas. He felt certain that the taciturn shifter would protect Zoe at all costs, and Bez's mate Sariel was a sweetheart of a woman. Not that the other mated females were anything less, but

Sariel had a natural mothering instinct that Deus sensed Zoe would appreciate.

Plus, Bez was a beast of a man who hunted and killed the worst of their kind. Who had taken on a fucking werewolf and lived to tell the tale. Twice. Deus wanted a soldier between his mate and the outside world if he couldn't be by her side. That described Bez to a tee.

Zoe didn't seem to like the idea, though. "Deus, no. If I'm leaving, you should come with me."

By the fates, his name sounded so good in her breathy voice. His cock practically wept at the sound, but he had to ignore the lust shooting through him. Had to put Zoe's safety first. He also had an Alpha who needed him. "I can't leave just yet—Luc needs me to help him figure out what's going on with this pack. And you heard Rudkin— there are two females somewhere in these woods who likely need us to get them out of here. I know you want me to stay with you, but I can't leave my brother or those women behind. And I won't be able to concentrate if I'm constantly worried about you or if the pack is going to come back and give us *three* females to hunt down. I won't risk your safety, Zoe. Not today, not ever. So, you go and I stay. I just need to alert the pilot that you're leaving and get your ass on the plane."

Zoe shook her head, clinging to his arms. "I want to stay with you."

He kissed her forehead, wishing they could just go back to the cabin again and spend some hours lost in one another. Knowing there was no way. "It's too dangerous. I will not risk your freedom that way. I know you're not happy about it, but please agree to get on that plane. Let me send you someplace safe where my brothers can take care of you. I won't be able to focus if I think there's any way these fuckers can get their grubby paws on you."

"You don't want me to go home."

Deus paused, looking up at her, making sure she understood the seriousness of his words. "I want you safe. This...this was too much. It will take days for my wolf to settle, and I won't have you with me during the process. I want to send you to Dire Wolf Bez—he has a sweet mate who I think you'll like and a big, guarded property in Texas. You'll be about as far away from this pack as you can get without leaving the country."

"And what about you?"

He'd be missing her every second of the day. "I'll come for you as soon as I can."

The sad sort of look in her eyes gutted him, as did the softness of her voice as she asked, "Promise?"

"Promise. And you don't have to stay there if you hate it. I need to know you're away from here and safe, but if you choose to leave Texas, it's okay. I don't care where you go—I'll track you down. I'll never let you go unless you push me away."

She sighed, big and loud and exaggerated. "Fine. I'll go to fucking Texas. Next time, can we make it an island somewhere with cabana boys?"

"Island, yes. You in a bikini, fuck yes. Cabana boys, no. We'll work out the details once this job is over."

"Fine. Now, let's get me out of Alaska."

His wolf made a plaintive sound as he set her down just inside the hangar. The smell of the other wolves permeated the space, putting every one of his instincts on alert, but he could tell they were alone. Something he needed to change no matter how much he hated the idea of another man coming anywhere near his mate. And he especially hated the idea of another man around her while she was in the state she was—naked.

Fuck, Deus loved her naked.

"You need a cloak," he said, his voice far too deep. "I have to call the pilot out here."

Her head cock accentuated the length of her neck and the curve of her shoulders. "Won't he think it odd that I'd be wearing nothing but a cloak?"

Deus snarled and grabbed her again, tugging her into his body. Rubbing himself against her and making sure his scent coated her skin. "He won't know. And if he's smart, he won't even fucking look your way."

"Such a caveman."

He tweaked one of her nipples as he grunted a harsh, "Mine."

She rolled her eyes at his possessiveness, but there was no denying her grin. She liked him as a caveman. "I'll find something to cover what's yours." Her dark eyes ran up and down the length of him, pausing as she took in his very large, very hard cock. "And what's mine."

Hers. Always. His wolf chuffed, proud to be called hers. Deus couldn't focus on that, though. He needed to call the pilot, set up Zoe's trip to Texas, and keep her safe until she was in the air and away from the Brooks Range pack. So as Zoe padded through the hangar, digging in boxes and turning up her nose at the mess therein, Deus headed to the office in the far corner. Two phone calls and one transfer of a ridiculous amount of money later, Deus had a pilot on his way to the hangar and a Dire Wolf brother preparing his home to welcome their newest member. Thank fuck for Bez and Sariel.

He'd just hung up the phone after locking in Zoe's flight details with Bez when the woman herself walked into the room. She had covered herself in what looked as if it had once been a simple, tan raincoat but that she'd turned into a sexy-as-fuck dress with a plunging neckline and a slit showing off way too much thigh for others to see. For him? It wasn't nearly enough.

He sat back in his chair, rubbing his thumb over the corner of his mouth as he looked her up and down. "Not sure that's much better than being naked, Beautiful."

"You can use my name now, you know."

"I do, but you'll always be my Beautiful." He crooked a finger at her. "Get over here, mate."

"So bossy."

But she came. And he'd make sure she was well rewarded for that.

"We've got forty-five minutes," he said as he tugged her into his lap. Zoe spread her legs over his, straddling him and giving him a peek at the pussy he hadn't gotten a taste of in far too long.

"That's it?" She placed her hands on his chest and pouted her bottom lip. "I was hoping for a little more time."

Yeah, so was he. And yet he needed her out of the state. Needed to know she was safe so he could take care of his Alpha and finish the job he'd been assigned. Still…forty-five minutes wasn't very long for all he wanted to do.

There wasn't a second to waste.

Deus slid his hands under the coat-dress Zoe wore and dragged her up his thighs, rocking his hips into her once he had her settled over his cock. Teasing her as he growled.

"I can do a lot in that time."

"Prove it."

So he did.

Twenty-One

A week without Deus was far more taxing than Zoe cared to admit. She worried about him endlessly, especially since he'd gone radio silent the second she'd made it to Texas. One text was all she received after she'd let him know she'd landed.

Be careful. Going into the wild and won't be able to text. Call this number if you need anything.

He'd left a phone number, one she didn't recognize. One Sariel—mate of the man who was supposed to be her guard—said belonged to another member of their pack. He'd sent her to one brother and given her the contact info of another just in case. He truly must have trusted these shifters.

She hadn't called the number, though. Hadn't felt comfortable being around his pack without him there either. Sariel had seemed nice, but the man...Bez. He unnerved her with his ice-like stare and harsh voice. She'd lasted a whole three days before taking off for New York, something that had caused Bez to offer her the first smile she'd seen on his face.

"Deus deserves a woman like you," he'd said. Zoe still wasn't sure if that was a compliment or not, but she didn't care. She'd made it back to New York, back to the city where she could disappear, where she could stroll through her neighborhood and feel confident in her safety. Where she could revisit the coffee shop where she'd first met her mate and wallow in how much she missed his scent. Which was what she was doing...wallowing and waiting. At the same table where they'd met. With a cup of tea on her hands just like the first time. She was fully aware of how pathetic the entire situation made her seem to the average person. She also gave no shits about it. She missed her mate and found the coffee shop comforting.

Still, being alone and not knowing if Deus was safe tore her up inside. With every passing day, she grew that much closer to flying back to Alaska to find him or calling the number in her phone to see if the voice on the other end knew anything about what was going on. She wanted Deus home, wanted to see him and feel him and...complete her mating bond to him. She'd never thought she'd give in to such an instinct, but with Deus, the choice was easy. He'd come for her when she'd needed him, said all the words she'd always dreamed of hearing from a man, and he'd practically worshiped her body as he'd whispered all his promises and vows. She couldn't have asked for a better mate, and she wasn't going to let him get away.

But she needed him to come home before she could lock that down.

"Excuse me. Are you waiting for someone?"

Zoe looked up at the strange man before her. Tall, blond, handsome in that overly polished sort of way—he had a smile that probably got a lot of attention from women.

Before Deus, she might have returned the look, might have flirted a bit. Might have even agreed to a date or two if she liked the way the conversation went. This was not before-Deus time, though.

"Yes, I am."

He gave her a smile, one that seemed charming enough but did nothing for her. "Any man would be a fool to keep a beautiful woman like you waiting."

And any man who tried to get between her and her mate would be wasting his time, but she didn't say that. Instead, she grabbed her tea, bringing it to her lips as a distraction. As a reminder to herself of how good it felt to be kissed by Deus. "Some things are more important than beauty."

He didn't argue her point. One last sip as the man walked away, then Zoe was up and headed for the door. It was time to quit lamenting her missing lover and get to work. Evening had begun to settle in, the shadows deepening as her time in the coffee shop had passed. Just as she'd wanted them to. She needed to set aside thoughts of Deus for a few hours. She had a job to do—a snatch and grab of a ring in a private home. An alarmed, guarded private home. The challenge had intrigued her from the start, and the fact that the payout would be higher than any job she'd done in recent years had her practically salivating to earn that money. Fifteen minutes…all she needed was fifteen minutes and a little skill. Then she could lament her missing mate some more but with a much fuller bank account.

Zoe had a lot of time on her hands—might as well make some money while she waited for Deus to show back up.

Dressed to blend into the shadows, Zoe made her way down the street behind the house where she'd been directed for the job. She'd been staking out the place for two days, watching for patterns in the people who worked there, looking for the best way inside. She'd found it quite by accident—a cat she'd startled had shown a breach in the house's security. A rat could fit through a hole the size of a quarter, a mouse one the size of a dime. Cats needed a bit more space, but not so much that a dog couldn't follow them depending on breed and size.

Dog…or wolf.

Zoe cut through a yard and headed into the alley, angling her way toward her destination. She kept herself out of sight of the house right up until she stood close enough to touch it. Gangways between buildings were wonderful things— dark and quiet and rarely utilized. Unless someone needed to get to the wires leading inside the house.

It took her two minutes to disable the alarm system, another three to slip inside a basement window that had been left unlocked at some point. The one the cat had been using to get in and out. She'd had to partially shift to make it through the small space, but she'd done it. Barely.

The hair on the back of her neck stood on end as she worked her way up the stairs toward the first-floor library where she'd been told the ring would be stored. She sensed a presence in the house, one that was just far enough away for her not to get a good scent of. No one was supposed to be home at this hour, but there would be a guard on property. She assumed that was the person she sensed, and she did *not* want to run into him.

Quick, quick, quick. Get it done and get out.

She kept her steps soft and light, kept her body tucked against the walls in case someone surprised her. And yet, everything about the job felt easy. Too easy. Too simple, even. So she crept, and she fought to keep her heart from pounding out of her chest, and she let her wolf senses absorb as much as she could without shifting.

Still just the one presence. Still no scent. Still too easy to be safe.

Zoe made it to the darkened library without a sound, and without running into the guard either. As expected, the ring sat at the far end of the space in a glass case lit from above. The entire display made the ring appear to be a showpiece, something much more valued than simply for the stones and metal. Something that made the owner proud. Whether that was due to family history or some other sort of legend regarding the piece, Zoe didn't care. She wasn't being paid to care. She was being paid to retrieve the piece, so she would.

Still, the ring felt like more than a simple piece of jewelry to her. She could see the sparks from where she stood, could practically sense the weight of it in her palm. Just a few more minutes, and she'd have it. She'd be close enough to figure out why she couldn't look away from it. Once she snatched that gorgeous bauble, she could get the hell out of there. She simply needed to take the ring, retrace her steps to the broken window in the basement, and disappear into the night. Almost done. Almost payday.

She crossed the library slowly, keeping an eye out for any sort of trap or sensor that would give her away. Nothing appeared obvious, but she still worried. Still fought her instincts that said something wasn't right about this job. Fought to ignore the wolf chanting in her head. *Too easy, too easy, too—*

The lights popped on, and she spun, ready to run, to defend herself. To shift if she needed to.

"Go ahead." Deus stood in the corner, smiling at her. Watching her. Zoe's heart pounded louder, her wolf's chant turning to a joyous howl. The beast practically danced on tiptoe, thrilled to be reunited with her mate. Zoe wanted to run to him, to throw herself into his arms and rub her scent all over him. But she stood stock-still, waiting. Knowing he had his own plans for her. Wanting to see what they were.

Deus' smile grew as he watched her struggle. "Take it, Zoe. That's what you're here for."

"And if I don't?"

He pushed off the wall, keeping his eyes on hers and stalking closer. "Then I won't get to ask you the question I've been obsessing over for the past seven days."

By the fates, the man was going to kill her. Breathing hard, unable to keep her hands from shaking, she closed the distance between herself and the prize. She lifted the glass enclosure and set it on the floor before reaching out for the ring. She'd been right about the weight of it—there would be no forgetting about a ring such as this for the wearer. The feel of it in her hand soothed her, though. Felt right. And the ring...gorgeous. White gold or platinum, hard to tell, with a cushion-cut stone that positively gleamed. A total stunner, and a perfect piece in her opinion.

She tore her eyes away from the ring to watch Deus as he sauntered her way. He looked hungry and impatient, something she liked. Something that reminded her of sin and sex and lust. And he looked like her mate. To the end of time, no matter what happened, he would always be hers. She couldn't wait to make that official. To tell him what she wanted. But Deus seemed focused on the ring, so she waited. When he finally reached her, he grabbed her hand, plucking the ring from her palm before lacing their fingers together. Holding on tight.

"It's a human custom, I'm aware. But I like the idea of you wearing something that carries a claim in their world." His smile turned cocky, his grip on her tightening. "Something that states my ownership of you."

She fought back the urge to grab his face and kiss the fuck out of him. She also fought back the instinct to smack that arrogant grin off his lips. "No one owns me, Alaska."

"Oh, I know that well, my beautiful mate. But I still like to think of you as mine." Deus leaned in, planting his lips on hers and stealing a kiss that rocked her down to her toes. Whining, whimpering in the back of her throat, she clung to him as he licked his way inside and claimed her mouth. Hand on her ass, grip pulling her against him until she felt how hard and thick he was for her, Deus didn't let up. He kissed her until she completely broke for him, until she wobbled and trembled with her need to be naked with him. With her desire to be filled by him. Taken by him. Claimed by him.

When he had her just as wild and out of control as he wanted her, Deus pulled away, dropping his voice into a husky, sensual sort of murmur that sent shock waves right to her clit. "Be mine, Zoe. Forever. Human world, shifter world—I don't care so long as you're by my side. Officially. If you're not ready for a full claiming, let me give you this. The human equivalent."

She didn't care about human anything in that moment, though. All she cared about—all she could focus on—was that her mate was back. And she hadn't known he was coming. "Where have you been?"

He huffed a laugh. "I knew you wouldn't make things easy on me."

"Deus—"

"There's trouble with that pack in Alaska. We've been following them to try to get a bead on where they've stashed their females."

"Did you find them?"

"Not yet."

"Which means you have to go back."

"Yes, in a few days. I would have stayed, but Levi needed to get back to his mate, so Luc let me come home until we could replace him."

"Levi?"

"Another Dire Wolf. He's been following you since you left Texas."

That…disturbed her and yet comforted her at the same time. He'd cared enough to have her tracked. "You sent someone to watch me?"

"Yes." Straightforward. Confident. Unruffled by her obvious disbelief. Typical Deus.

"Why?"

"Because you're my mate. I understood your desire to be home, which was why I'd told Bez never to stand in your way. But that doesn't mean I wasn't worried about you."

"I don't need a bodyguard."

"No, you need someone to prove they'll be there for you, and you need a ring on your finger to stop humans like the man at the coffee shop from thinking they have a chance." He grabbed her hand and flipped it over, showing her the ring again. "I intend to give you both."

"You saw that?"

"Yes, through their security feed. I almost felt bad for the poor guy—you looked spectacular as you sat there all distracted and alone. Now, quit stalling. Give me an answer, Zophiel. Tell me if you'll be mine the way I want to be yours."

Zoe couldn't breathe. This was all so much and not enough. She wanted him more than anything, wanted forever at his side. Wanted the freedom that came with being claimed by a man like him. She'd never wanted anything more. So she stopped running away from her destiny.

"What if I want more?"

He frowned. "More diamonds?"

"No, more of you. What if I want it all?"

Deus blinked, his eyes growing darker. More wolflike. More animalistic. "Be specific. What is it you want?"

"You. Me. Mated." Zoe rose on the balls of her feet to get closer to him, keeping her hands braced on his chest as she whispered, "Claim me, mate."

Deus growled, his eyes turning silver. A sign of his Dire

Wolf coming closer to the surface of his mind. Something she'd studied all week while she'd been missing him. Something that made her tremble inside with a strange sexual sort of fear. He was so much more than just a wolf shifter, so dominant and powerful, and she couldn't wait to explore what all that meant. How strong he could be when they were together. How strong he would love her in the coming years.

How deep she would fall for him once they were tied together forever.

Deus grabbed her by the hips and tugged her against him, his voice somewhere close to a gravelly rumble as he said, "Mine now. All mine."

She was. And she always would be. A thought which should have sent her running the other way, but she knew he would be hers just as much. He'd never force her into anything because he liked it when she called the shots. And she'd never be helpless again because she already knew how to stand on her own feet and fight for herself. Their mating might not have been as traditional as some, but she had a feeling it would work for them.

Hell, he might even like it if she ordered him around a little. Zoe figured it was a good time to find out.

"Show me how much," she said, rubbing her body against his the way she'd been wanting to since she first saw him. Scenting him as hers. "Mark me, Deus. Claim me."

He had her on the floor before she could blink, had her naked seconds later. Skin-on-skin, his warmth bleeding into her, he kissed every inch of her body, never letting go or backing away. Covering her right there on the library floor of her mark. *Shit.*

"We can't," she gasped, hating herself for even saying the words. "Not here."

"We can." He bit her nipple, causing her to buck, his

heavy cock sliding to her entrance with the motion. "My Alpha owns this place. The job was a setup to get you here. Don't worry—you'll still get paid."

"Oh." She arched her back, angling to make him slide inside her. Wanting to feel him deep. "That was an asshole move, but I get it. And you should really up your security."

"We'll pay you to work on that for us." He chuckled and rocked his hips, teasing her with his cock. Giving her the tip before backing away. "Are you ready for me, mate?"

Mate. That word made her body pulse with need for him, made her legs wrap themselves around him as if of their own volition. That word meant everything to her... and she had a feeling it would be the same for him. "I've been ready, *mate.*"

Deus thrust inside, one solid push embedding himself deep within her as he snarled out her name. Filling her with his body as he gave her everything he had. Zoe let him take a few minutes to find his rhythm, lifted her hips and fucked him back until he was a growling, sweating mess pounding into her. Then she raised her head, and she bit him right on the side of the neck. Breaking the skin and joining them forever in blood. Mating him.

Deus howled at the bite, his thrusts becoming uneven and rough, his head dropping down to return the bite. Claiming her as his as he fucked her across the floor. Their bond completed, she instantly felt more of him inside of her, sensed his essence and emotions along with her own, his pure love for her. His feelings ricocheted through and around hers, but Zoe focused on her own. On sending them his way. Making sure her love for him, her trust in him, was strong and true. Wanting him to feel just as much, to understand. To know that she meant it when she said she was his. Always.

They came together in a climax that left them both

breathless and clingy. That rocked Zoe to the center of her soul and reset her perceptions of the entire world. At least for that moment. Right there on the floor, blood and sweat and come all mingling together, they held each other and let their newfound connection grow. Let it build. Let it tie them to one another for all eternity. Zoe finally understood why pack wolves took a Klunzad period. She could have lain with Deus forever in their post-mating afterglow.

At least until her hips started to complain about the hard floor underneath her. "Hey, Alaska?"

"Yeah, Beautiful?"

"Next time you feel the need to give me a claiming bite, let's make sure there's a bed nearby."

He sat back, lifting his weight off her but giving her a lazy, satisfied sort of grin. "Next time?"

"Yeah." She licked up the length of his neck, right over the bite she'd given him. Over the spot she couldn't stop staring at. *Hers.* He was all hers. "I have a feeling I'm going to be marking your body for years to come."

He rolled her on top of him, looking up at her with eyes filled with a devotion she could *feel.* "Mark me however you want. I'm yours."

Zoe leaned down to press a soft kiss on his lips before rocking her hips to take him inside her once more. To start their mating all over again. "And I'm yours. So, take me, mate. Show me how much you need me."

And he did. Many times. Though they never did make it to a bed that night.

Epilogue

*D*eus woke suddenly, the jerking of the plane as it landed pulling him from sleep without warning. The NYC skyline glittered far outside the window, but there. Right there. Fuck, it was good to be back on the East Coast. One more hour, maybe two if traffic sucked as much as he knew it could, and he'd be home. Back in the penthouse apartment he loved so much. The one he'd also begun to hate as the weeks had flown past. Not because the space had changed, but that he had. He'd found his fated mate—a woman who was just as independent after he'd claimed her as she had been before. And no matter how much he loved his neighborhood and apartment, if Zoe wasn't in the space, he didn't want to be there. The woman had been insistent on keeping her own place and dragging them back and forth based on whatever whims she seemed to have. She drove him crazy, and he loved every second of it.

The plane taxied into the hanger, and Deus hopped to his feet, heading for the door before they'd come to a full stop. It'd been eight days since he'd seen his mate. Eight long, lonely days of failure and frustration as he'd trekked all over the Brooks Range area with his Alpha in search of two women he couldn't be sure even existed. Two women no one outside of the elusive pack in the area had ever seen.

But he'd put in his time and had waited as patiently as possible for another Dire brother to take over for him. All six Dires in the lower forty-eight were taking turns in the wilderness to help Luc search for the missing women. Two at a time, they'd fly up to Alaska, spend a week or so in the woods, then fly home as the next duo arrived. This had been his second trip up there, the entire Dire Wolf pack focusing on Luc's obsession with finding these women instead of anything coming in from the NALB. The pressure to succeed, to calm their Alpha and give him what he obviously needed, had gotten intense. Deus didn't know how much longer they could all keep going.

He'd also begun to wonder if there was something special about these women. Something that called to Luc's wolf the way Zoe called to his. If his Alpha had somehow gotten close enough to his fated mate to sense their connection and was now seeking her out without even realizing it. That's what fueled Deus to keep looking, to spend so much time away from his new mate—the idea that his Alpha had almost found his fated mate but would lose her before he ever met her. That sort of torture—the mental anguish of it all—could drive a wolf mad. No way could Deus leave Luc to that fate. No way any of the Dire brothers could.

So they hunted, and they followed Luc down whatever dark path his senses took them. And they all hoped for a positive outcome. Soon.

Carl, the pilot Deus preferred to fly with, came out of the cockpit and grabbed the handle to open the door of the plane, likely knowing how anxious his one passenger was to get the fuck out of the metal tube. "See you in a week?"

By the fates, he hoped not. "Probably. I'll call the service and set up anything I need."

"Of course, sir. Enjoy your time with your wife."

Wife. Okay, that word made Deus smile for the first time in over a week. His wife. He'd locked that shit down—had dragged Zoe to a courthouse and let a judge tell them some contract would join them for life. They both knew what a joke that was in comparison to their fated connection, but the piece of paper meant something to Deus. And thank the fates, he meant something to her, so she obliged him the human custom.

Deus pulled his phone out as soon as he got into the back of the car he'd hired to take him home and sent his mate a text. Nothing too detailed, a simple *on my way home*, but he expected a response. He didn't get one. The longer the car ride lasted, the more he fidgeted. The more he wanted to send another text, to call Zoe so he could hear her voice. Wanted to pull up his tracking app to find her. He didn't, though. He waited. She knew he was coming home tonight, knew he'd want to see her. She'd show up...when she was ready.

By the time he reached his building, the need for his mate and irritation at how long it took to make the way across town had soured his mood. He needed something to eat, a little time in front of the game he hadn't been able to play in weeks, a good fifteen hours of sleep, and his mate. Not necessarily in that order. He even took the elevator to the top floor—something he almost never did—instead of climbing the stairs. Anything to get to his apartment faster.

But when he opened the door to his place, all that stress and worry and irritation disappeared. Zoe's scent permeated the air, and he could hear the telltale sounds of her gaming in the living room. His mate was waiting for him. Or not waiting, as it seemed.

"Playing without me?" he called out, heading toward the wall of screens. Toward the heaven he knew to be waiting for him. Toward the gift he'd been given by the fates—the woman of his dreams wrapped in a hot-as-fuck shewolf's body. His girl was worth the thousand-year wait.

"I've been playing without you for a week. A girl has needs, you know." Zoe's soft chuckle made his heart jump, and the sight of her bare leg draped over the arm of his chair—of her foot bouncing up and down—had his cock hardening and his wolf alert. He couldn't get to her fast enough, couldn't wait to touch all that skin and taste every inch. But she stopped him in his tracks with a mere six words.

"I've moved in, by the way."

Dead. Stop. In the best way. "Moved in?"

She spun the chair around, giving him a view of her naked body. Of her resting his favorite gaming keyboard across her silky thighs in some sort of computer geek fantasy image he would never forget. Ever. Fuck, the woman had style.

"Yes, moved in. As in, left my place and had all my things brought here." Her lips kicked up in a smile that rocked him to his soul. "I assumed you wouldn't mind."

"Mind?" Deus dropped his bag and stripped out of his clothes, shredding the fastenings of his jeans in the process. Too impatient to take the time to do things right. He had a naked mate to take care of and a cock that needed to be inside her. Denim didn't matter. "I think that's the best thing I've heard since you said 'I do.'"

"I figured as much. I would have had your stuff moved to my place, but it was time for me to move on anyway. The humans were getting nosy."

"That's why I like buildings without a doorman."

"But who will hold my hand and help me out of the

car?"

"Me." Deus couldn't hold back his quiet growl as he slipped into the chair behind her, settling her on his lap. "You don't need help getting out of the car though."

"No, but I like to feel cared for."

"I'll care for you." He reached around and grabbed her breasts, massaging gently, tweaking her nipples for good measure before slipping one hand down her stomach to cup her between her legs. "I'll care for you real good, starting with this needy pussy. Have you missed me, Beautiful?"

She shifted against him, positioning herself so his fingers were *right there*. So he could feel how wet she already was. "Every second."

"Is that why you finally decided to move in here?" Because she hadn't wanted to. Not even after the claiming bites they'd exchanged or the wedding vows. Deus had assumed she'd needed a backup plan—to feel she could escape if necessary. She'd had another late-night incident like the one in Alaska. Had woken up and been half trapped in her own mind as she'd eaten almost everything in the kitchen. Deus had simply kept her company, handing her food when she needed it, staying still and silent when she didn't. He hated seeing her so anxious and afraid, but thankfully, he'd been there with her. The very idea that she'd have an episode when he couldn't be there haunted him when he was away. At least if she lived with him, he could make sure the kitchen was well stocked. That she wouldn't run out of food when she needed it most. That she wouldn't be alone when the darkness of her memories took over.

Fuck, he never wanted to leave her side again.

"I decided to move in here because you have a better view than I do," she said, sounding snarky and sure. Teasing him. That at least settled his worries a little.

It also gave him the chance to tease right back. "And

better takeout. The Cantonese place by you had crap egg rolls."

"Didn't stop you from eating ten of them."

"I'm a man with a big appetite, as you well know." Deus chuckled, holding her tight. So damn thankful to feel her against him once more. Never wanting to let her go. "Fuck me, Beautiful. I don't ever want to leave you again."

Zoe gripped his arm, dragging his hand up her body to kiss his wrist. "But you'll have to soon again, I bet."

He would. They both knew it. Until they found the women Luc seemed obsessed about, all the Dire Wolves would be taking extended trips to Alaska. Hell, even Michaela—Phego's doctor mate—had been recruited to be there, just in case they needed her skills. At least she and Phego could stay together, though. Deus had to leave Zoe behind, and he hated it more than he'd ever hated anything in his life.

"We've got a week before that happens. And who knows—if Luc finds these women, maybe I won't have to go back up."

Zoe hummed. "Too bad. I was thinking that a nice, long weekend in a cabin on some snowy mountain might be a nice way to spend our Klunzad."

"I thought that week we spent right here was our Klunzad?" The week after he'd gotten back from his first trip to Alaska. The week when they'd become husband and wife. The week when he'd fucked her on just about every surface of his apartment before flying across the country once more. That had been a great week.

Apparently, Zoe thought so as well. "Are you saying you don't want a repeat?"

"I'm not even close to saying that." Deus bit down on her neck—not breaking the skin, but holding her in place just for a moment before pulling back so he could lick the sting away. "We can start our repeat Klunzad week right now. What do you want, mate? My hand, my cock, my tongue? What can I do to show you how much I've missed every inch of you?"

Zoe groaned and rocked against his hand, gripping his thighs for leverage. "I figured you'd want to relax with your game here."

His game. Literally. The one he'd designed. The one they liked to play together sometimes. Fuck, she really was perfect for him, and yet... "We can play that later. Right now, I want to play with my favorite toy."

"So now I'm your toy?"

"Correction—my *favorite* toy." With a rock of his hips and his hands holding her hips, Deus slid inside Zoe's tight, wet heat. Fuck, coming home had never felt so good. So right. No way would he ever give this up, would he ever risk his connection with her. He'd feed her, care for her, make sure she had everything she needed and the life she wanted... as long as she stayed beside him.

As long as she was his.

As long as she let him be hers.

"Ride me, Beautiful. I want to feel you come on my cock."

So she did. A few times. Deus had a feeling he'd get a Klunzad week every time he came home from a mission. Didn't make him want to leave her, though. Nothing ever would.

Coming soon from *USA Today*
bestselling author Ellis Leigh...
SAVAGE SALVATION
the explosive conclusion to the
Devil's Dires series.

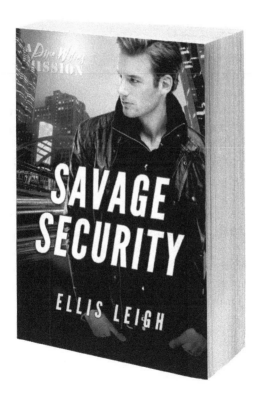

A *Dire Wolves* MISSION

Acknowledgments

There are a lot of emotions that go with this book. See, I was writing it in late 2016 when chaos exploded all around me. The words died quickly, and I struggled with focus and attention. Out of that time came London Hale, a pen name meant to distract us all from the dumpster fire around us. It took me over a year to be able to come back to this world, over a year to find my footing as Ellis once more and dig deep.

Thanks to Brighton for dragging my ass back from the brink of despair. Thanks to Lisa for giving me the freedom to take the time I needed to tell Deus' story. Thanks to my Bitches for keeping me sane. Thanks to Heather for never flouncing me even when we disagreed on things. Thanks to my readers for being patient with me. Just…thanks.

About
the Author

A storyteller from the time she could talk, *USA Today* bestsellng author Ellis Leigh grew up among family legends of hauntings, psychics, and love spanning decades. Those stories didn't always have the happiest of endings, so they inspired her to write about real life, real love, and the difficulties therein. From farmers to werewolves, store clerks to witches—if there's love to be found, she'll write about it. Ellis lives in the Chicago area with her husband, daughters, and to tiny fish that take up way too much of her time.

www.ellisleigh.com

A *Dire Wolves* MISSION

Printed in the USA
CPSIA information can be obtained
at www.ICGtesting.com
LVHW051255240124
769536LV00003B/386

9 781944 336523